To André

ONE

December 1997

It was Mary Kellick who first stumbled upon the grisly scene. Of course it had to be Mary—tense, anxious Mary—who was first to see the waxen corpse. She had heard somewhere—or had she read it?—that there was a great deal of blood in a body, and now she saw it was true. There was blood everywhere—gallons, she thought—seeping into the thick white carpet.

Questioned by the police, she could remember only the blood. "Nothing there," commented Detective Chief Inspector Hay following the interview, to no one in particular. Not that it mattered. The experts had been on the scene quickly enough with their cameras, plastic bags, and paper envelopes. The corpse was that of a woman in her mid-forties. Her throat had been slashed, and she lay gaping at the ceiling with dark, vacant eyes. She had been identified by Sergeant Roy Carpenter, the High Commission's junior liaison officer for the Royal Canadian Mounted Police.

The venue was curious and troubling. The Official Residence of the Canadian High Commissioner in London was an unexpected site for violent crime. The body had been found in an anteroom off the main dining hall. The anteroom was richly appointed but too small to accommodate the entire investigation team at once. While the first few experts got to work, the rest of the team waited impatiently in the dining room, which was enormous and flanked by expensive oil paintings. It had space, thought Hay, for some forty well-heeled diners.

Mary Kellick, the High Commissioner's engagements secretary, had been unable to identify the victim. She said that she had been doing her usual nightly rounds, sometime between nine and nine-thirty, when she came across the body. There had been no official function that night—the High Commissioner and his wife were in Scotland—or her rounds would have begun later. No, Kellick had heard nothing at all beforehand. She had been in her small apartment, which was adjacent to the Residence, and Hay allowed her to return there at the end of their talk.

A QUIET KILL

A FORSYTH AND
HAY MYSTERY

A QUIET KILL

JANET BRONS

TouchWood
Editions

TouchWood Editions
touchwoodeditions.com

LIBRARY AND ARCHIVES CANADA CATALOGUING IN PUBLICATION
Brons, Janet, 1954–, author
A quiet kill / Janet Brons.

Issued in print and electronic formats.
ISBN 978-1-77151-060-8

I. Title.

PS8603.R653Q54 2014   C813'.6   C2013-905948-2

Editor: Frances Thorsen
Proofreader: Cailey Cavallin
Design: Pete Kohut
Cover image: Hammondovi, istockphoto.com
Fog texture: elisafox.deviantart.com
Author photo: © Lindsay-Mae Photography

We gratefully acknowledge the financial support for our publishing activities
from the Government of Canada through the Canada Book Fund, Canada
Council for the Arts, and the province of British Columbia through the
British Columbia Arts Council and the Book Publishing Tax Credit.

The interior pages of this book have been printed on 30% post-consumer
recycled paper, processed chlorine free, and printed with vegetable-based inks.

1 2 3 4 5 18 17 16 15 14

PRINTED IN CANADA

Mary Kellick sat at her kitchen table. She stared at the cheery blue and white checks on the tablecloth, purchased when French country had been in vogue. All the magazines and lifestyle programs had pronounced, "Accented with yellow, this look is reminiscent of a lovely summer's day in Provence." Instead, it was a drizzling night in London, and Mary felt nauseous. She had been horrified by the sight of the body in the anteroom and all that blood. All that blood matted in the poor woman's long auburn hair . . . Mary started violently. It had to be Natalie. It was Natalie Guévin, the head of the High Commission's trade section, who was lying on the anteroom floor. She had been virtually unrecognizable. Mary suddenly realized that she was trembling uncontrollably and very, very cold.

RCMP Sergeant Roy Carpenter stood officiously just inside the anteroom, monitoring the comings and goings of the forensics team and documenting the removal of the various exhibits. He thought that the Deputy High Commissioner, Paul Rochon, had made a mistake inviting the British cops to the Residence so quickly. Carpenter knew that Rochon had contacted High Commissioner Carruthers, who was on holiday in Edinburgh, and that the decision had been made jointly. But a special detachment of the RCMP was being dispatched from Ottawa. Surely the crime scene could have waited. It was, after all, technically on Canadian soil—something called extraterritoriality. He wondered randomly whether Rochon might just have been squeamish about the body remaining on the premises any longer than absolutely necessary.

Carpenter, a tall, fit officer who prided himself on his daily ten-mile runs, was rather distrustful of the diminutive, narrow-shouldered Rochon with his pasty face. Rochon always made Carpenter a bit uncomfortable—and Carpenter's own discomfort made him feel, in turn, a bit guilty. He always found it strange to see the cadaverous Rochon, with his long, nervous fingers and that weak chin—why didn't the man at least grow a beard?—riding around in the official vehicle with the flag waving whenever the High Commissioner went back to Canada or otherwise left the UK. But Rochon was, after all, the number two, and that was just how it worked.

Although he believed he had a strong stomach—he had been in Bosnia, hadn't he?—Carpenter was content to busy himself by asking questions of the forensics team and taking notes. The state of the corpse was appalling. Anyway, he needed to be in a position to report fully to his own people when they arrived from Ottawa. Sergeant Carpenter stopped one of the junior police officers who was exiting the anteroom, and demanded to know what was in the plastic bag.

The few Residence staff who still "lived in" had been summarily roused from their evening rituals. A matched set of constables had woken the butler / part-time chauffeur from an early night's sleep; disturbed the chief cook from a televised football match; and, apparently, interrupted a somewhat flustered maid in her bath. All three expressed shock and disbelief over the murder, which was not surprising to the pair of young constables, both of whom believed themselves to have heard it all before.

Annie Mallett, the maid, was both horrified and thrilled by the events. She dried herself thoroughly, dressed quickly, and applied her makeup—complete with Violet Vixen lipstick. This could be an exciting night. She very much hoped that the detective chief inspector would look like that lovely Inspector Morse on television. Maybe she would be asked to look at the body. They might assign security guards to all their rooms. The newspapers might even want to interview her. The possibilities were endless.

Head Chef Luciano Alfredo Carillo was not pleased. Eight years in some of the finest cooking schools in Europe, executive chef in a top Swiss hotel, and now stuck working for these Canadians with their pedestrian palates. He had thought it would look good on his CV, but it had been a boring and frustrating couple of years. He sometimes wondered whether he was losing his passion for food as he wasted his talents on burgers and bran muffins for the Ambassador and his snob of a wife. Cooking for diplomatic functions was almost as bad: *this* one wouldn't eat pork, *that* one wouldn't eat beef, *she* was a vegetarian, *he* was allergic to shellfish . . . no wonder he felt his creativity being sapped. Tonight, however, with an absent High Commissioner and no functions to worry about, he had been enjoying the football match, which Manchester United was winning handily, and his bottle of Cabernet. Well, it wasn't his bottle exactly as it had originally been part of the High Commission stores, but Luciano Alfredo Carillo felt entitled to the odd liberty. And now he was being dragged out for some murder. As he pulled on his sweater, he suddenly had an unwelcome thought: was this murder perhaps a poisoning? He very much hoped not.

Anthony Thistlethwaite knotted his tie. He had been awakened from a delicious early-evening sleep by a knock on the door and two officious young constables announcing a murder. *Well, well,* he pondered, *in service in the Residence for thirty years and I thought I'd seen everything. Especially that cross-dressing fruitcake they sent here as High Commissioner a few years back. Kept complaining about the closet space. Or the time when that Kellick made a mess of the dinner invitations and twenty dignitaries, dressed to the nines, arrived at the Residence a week early. Now this. Well, well.*

The young constables reported back to DCI Hay that Mallett, Carillo, and Thistlethwaite were assembled and ready to be interviewed. "Tell Carpenter, will you?" said Hay. "He will want to be in on the interviews."

"He's a bit of a nosey parker, that one," muttered Constable Brent to his colleague.

Hay stiffened and raised his eyebrows. "A nosey parker you think, do you? This is technically Canadian soil. We are here at the invitation of the High Commission. You had best remember that."

Like many very tall men, Hay was imposing at the best of times, but when annoyed he could be positively intimidating. At least that was the young constable's opinion at the moment.

"Yes, sir. And, er, the Deputy High Commissioner should be arriving shortly. And," he repeated, trying to redeem himself, "we have collected the household staff for interviews. Sir." The last was uttered in a hopeful tone that served only to annoy Hay further.

"Bully for you," grumbled Hay as he strode back to the anteroom. "And Brent," he said, turning in mid-stride, "get Carpenter a cup of tea."

Deputy High Commissioner Paul Rochon sped toward the Official Residence, blinded by the reflection of oncoming headlights through the rain. He glanced at the gas gauge, remembering with annoyance that he was running low. He had meant to fill up the following morning, but then he could hardly have anticipated a murder at the Residence. It had been Carpenter, the RCMP liaison, who had called him at home, although it seemed that poor Mary Kellick had discovered the body. Smart kid, Mary, if terribly sensitive. Apparently she had been an excellent engagements secretary at one time but had become increasingly anxious and high strung in recent years. Sometimes she seemed nervous almost to the point of paralysis.

Paul's thoughts reverted to the matter at hand. He had contacted the High Commissioner at his hotel in Edinburgh without difficulty; the relief that he had experienced at hearing his boss's voice had been almost physical. Not that he was unaccustomed to making decisions and dealing with emergencies, but this was something altogether different. It was likely to become very complicated. Paul wondered vaguely if there was any precedent to such an event but doubted it very much. He was pleased to follow Wesley Carruthers's advice: phone the London Criminal Investigation Department, alert the Operations Centre in Ottawa, and request an RCMP team from Canada. Get to the High Commission. Alert the program heads. *No press.*

The High Commissioner had a cool head in a crisis. It had been a political appointment, as was usually the case in London, and Rochon had been prepared to dislike the newly minted High Commissioner Carruthers on sight. But the astute youngish former cabinet minister (Justice, wasn't it, followed by Environment?) made a surprisingly adept head of mission. Even Rochon, who had climbed steadily if not brilliantly through the ranks of the foreign service, had to admit that Carruthers possessed some excellent qualities, including a few not normally in the skill set of the average foreign service officer. For one, the High Commissioner got along remarkably well with the press and wasn't intimidated by them. As a former politician, he seemed to have accepted the credo that no publicity was bad publicity—except, at least for the moment, under the present circumstances. Many in the professional service, including Rochon, preferred to remain in the background and do their jobs with little or no fanfare. To have your name even mentioned in the press was not only embarrassing but often also a CLM—a "career-limiting move."

High Commissioner Carruthers also had a disarming way of making even complete strangers feel genuinely comfortable in his presence. He was generally very well-liked in the diplomatic community and, almost as important, by his own staff. His wife, of course, was another story. Sharon Carruthers seemed to take great pride in rubbing people the wrong way. Rochon wondered idly if she had any friends at all, then swerved quickly as a pedestrian appeared out of the darkness.

He turned the windshield wipers to full speed, and his thoughts turned to his earlier conversation with the Operations Centre in Ottawa. Some wittering old fool asking if Paul thought the deputy minister should be disturbed in Vancouver even for such news; after all, the DM *was* accompanying the minister at a very important conference, you know, and he hates to be bothered, especially for bad news . . . Rochon had hung up in frustration, leaving the old boy to his breakdown. Felt a bit bad about it now, of course, but honestly, if these are the guys you're supposed to call in a crisis . . .

This detective chief inspector did not look at all like Morse, thought Annie Mallett, sorely disappointed. He was very tall, with a thin face and a hawkish nose. Annie thought that he seemed somewhat sad. Quite a good head of white hair, though, so that was something.

She sat primly if somewhat uncomfortably at the dining room table, kitty-corner to Hay, who was seated at the head. Annie had dusted and polished this table often enough, but never before had she been seated there. She found the experience somewhat unsettling.

This end of the table had become something of an impromptu interview room. Already papers were littered about, and a junior constable had fetched coffee from down the street. The detective chief inspector, Annie noted, took his black, no sugar. A young detective sergeant was seated across from her with a small book, ready to take notes. He was much better-looking than his boss. If only she were thirty years younger, she thought with a small sigh.

She had been very surprised to learn that the victim was Natalie Guévin. There had been nothing at all mysterious about Natalie, nor had she even been particularly beautiful—well, at least not in a traffic-stopping sort of way. A rather unremarkable woman, Annie reckoned, to be killed in a fit of romantic passion or perhaps murdered as a pawn in a game of international espionage . . .

"So, Miss Mallett," the detective chief inspector broke into Annie's ruminations, "my name is Hay. I realize this is all rather upsetting. But can you tell me exactly where you were late this afternoon and this evening?" Hay leaned back, longing for a cigarette. The proliferation of stern No Smoking signs throughout the dining room served as an effective deterrent. He had understood from somewhere that Canadians in general were fanatical about not smoking. Anyway, he was situated close enough to the crime scene that he would run the risk of charges of contaminating evidence. Later, perhaps. He studied the peculiar-looking Annie Mallett, who had taken the time to apply a full makeup and might have spent the evening backcombing a mass of orange hair. She was staring intently at him and had adopted a jarringly coquettish manner.

Annie smoothed her skirt and thought very hard. "Well," she began, "after work, at three o'clock, I took the number four bus to the shops, didn't I? There's lots of good pre-Christmas sales on now, your wife might like to know," she said coyly. "I bought a bra"—here she coughed prettily—"and some sausage rolls from Marks & Spencer, didn't I? The cashier knows me—she can verify that," added Annie in a confidential tone.

Hay nodded, sighing inwardly. It was going to be a long night.

By the time the household staff was finished being interviewed, Hay had observed a good deal of the curious workings of a frustrated housemaid's mind, been subject to the sulks and tempers of an apparently unappreciated culinary *artiste*, and been treated by the butler-cum-chauffeur to a healthy dose of interesting but largely extraneous diplomatic gossip. He had learned little useful, except that all the live-ins claimed to have heard nothing at all unusual that evening. Hay found this peculiar. The living quarters were not all that far removed from the dining room, and the acoustics, in there at least, caused sound to echo and bounce alarmingly.

Three High Commission guards, two Canadians and a Scot, were interviewed, as was Sergeant Carpenter. The guards had neither seen nor heard anything unusual. It had been a relatively routine evening, except for the unusually high percentage of staff working late, doubtless due to the forthcoming visit of the Canadian foreign minister. No, staff departure times had not been logged: they never were. Arrivals and departures of visitors, however, were carefully monitored.

According to the guards, Mary Kellick had run shrieking into the guards' station at 9:25 PM. One of the guards had found her some brandy in the Canadian Club downstairs, which calmed her a little. The others immediately proceeded to investigate and secure the scene, and one had contacted Sergeant Carpenter at his home at 9:28. He, in turn, had alerted the Deputy High Commissioner, Paul Rochon. Carpenter corroborated the sequence of events, adding that he believed Rochon to have then contacted the High Commissioner in Scotland as well as Foreign Affairs in Ottawa.

Running his hands through his thick hair, Hay heartily wished that police work were nearly as exciting as Annie Mallett seemed to think it was. He signaled that he would see the acting High Commissioner now. The small, nervous-looking man had been standing by the entrance for some time. Paul Rochon was deathly white over what Hay assumed to be a normal pallor. He wore thick spectacles and, with trembling hands, gratefully accepted a cup of coffee.

Rochon told Hay of his earlier conversation with the High Commissioner and of the actions he had taken. Hay inquired as to when the RCMP team was expected on the ground. "With any luck, sir, later this morning." Hay realized with a start that it was already well past midnight. "Not, I mean," continued Rochon, "that we don't trust *your* lot. It's just that it *is* the High Commission, and . . . the deceased . . . *is* . . . or was, er, Canadian. You know."

"Yes, of course," agreed Hay, although privately he didn't really agree at all. This was the High Commission, but it was still in London, so surely that gave him some sort of jurisdiction? He was not clear on the diplomatic niceties, despite his earlier upbraiding of Constable Brent, and decided to tread carefully. Anyway, it might be amusing to

13

work with the Mounties for a while. Hay continued, "And you have been apprised of the identity of the victim?"

"Yes, the constable told me. I can't believe it. It must have been an intruder, a nutcase."

Hay doubted that very much but asked, "Did you know Ms. Guévin well?"

"Not very, at least not socially, if you know what I mean. We've worked together for about eighteen months, after she came in from a posting in Bangkok. I've been here for two years myself. She was an excellent officer."

"Married? Kids?"

"No. Divorced, I think. Never mentioned any kids."

"Did she have any particular friends here at the High Commission?"

"Not really. But then, none of us do. This isn't like a lot of posts, where the local environment sort of forces you together in a false camaraderie, if you know what I mean. Here you can get out, make local friends, make a life for yourself without the local security service breathing down your neck."

Detective Sergeant Richard Wilkins, who had been quietly taking interview notes, was pleased as always to be working with Detective Chief Inspector Hay, but found himself slightly out of his depth in this world of diplomacy. He was somewhat puzzled by the numerous references to the "High Commission." Finally he asked, "Excuse me, Mr. Rochon, but, for clarification, can you please tell me why this is called a 'High Commission'? I thought that diplomatic offices were 'Embassies'?"

Rochon smiled and nodded. "Yes, a lot of people are confused by that. Diplomatic premises from one Commonwealth country located in another Commonwealth country are called High Commissions; non-Commonwealth countries have Embassies. So while Canada has High Commissions in London and, say, Canberra, it would have an Embassy in, for instance, the US or Germany."

"Ah, okay, thanks."

Hay continued, "So there was no one, then, who might have known her a bit better than anyone else?"

"Well, come to think of it . . . she was a bit chummy with the military attaché, Colonel Lahaie. They used to ride together. Horses, that is." Rochon seemed to find horseback riding a somewhat frivolous pastime. "At Hyde Park, a couple of times a week, I think."

Rochon rehearsed his whereabouts that evening. Working at home on the forthcoming ministerial visit. Too many distractions at the office to concentrate, even in the evenings. A few phone calls to the UK desk at Foreign Affairs in Ottawa. A take-away vindaloo around seven. Then the phone call from Carpenter, around nine-thirty.

"Finally, Mr. Rochon, can you think of anyone who might have a motive to kill Ms. Guévin?"

Rochon hesitated perhaps a fraction of a second too long and then said decisively, "No. No one at all."

Forensics had helped the coroner's team prepare the body for transport to the morgue, and Dr. Shelly, the forensic pathologist, was waiting patiently for Hay to finish his interviews. If one learned anything in forensics, it was patience—and perhaps an ability to discriminate between the important and the trivial. Soon Hay was listening intently as Shelly—who had been called by the coroner to attend the scene—related his initial findings. The time of death appeared to be between roughly seven and eight in the evening, according to the victim's core warmth and level of lividity, or pooling of blood in the body. Cause of death was massive blood loss resulting from a deep cut to the throat, apparently following a severe blow to the back of the head. Either the carotid artery or the jugular had been severed, given the large quantity of blood at the scene.

The attack, according to Shelly, appeared to have been carried out by someone who knew exactly what he, possibly she, was doing. There was no obvious evidence of sexual interference, but this would have to be confirmed at autopsy. No defensive wounds on the woman's hands. A wooden club of some type had been left on the scene and had been bagged for analysis. There was no knife in sight.

"So she was clobbered before she had a chance to cry out. That explains why no one seems to have heard anything. No struggle—just taken by surprise."

"It looks that way. And even if the bashing she took didn't silence her, the knife did. Sliced straight through the vocal cords. By the way, the only way to achieve that sort of cut is if the attacker struck from behind. Of course we have further tests to run, but it seems pretty straightforward to me at this point."

Hay winced and stood up. He had been parked behind the dining hall table for several hours now, and his knee was starting to ache. "Well, Wilkins," he said quietly to his detective sergeant, "what do you think we have here?"

Watching as the woman's bagged body was wheeled into the corridor, DS Richard Wilkins could only shake his head and mutter, "I don't have any bloody idea, sir."

TWO

The High Commissioner's "no press" edict only remained in effect for about half an hour. Someone at Scotland Yard who owed a favor called a contact in a wire service, and soon the story was being reported in both Britain and Canada. The Canadian foreign affairs minister was surprised by the news at a press conference during the high-profile meeting in Vancouver. In front of the foreign press and observed by ministerial colleagues from around the globe, the minister was forced to admit that he had not heard about the murder on the premises of the High Commission in London. Shortly thereafter, a rather bewildered Operations Centre employee whose reaction time had not been quite up to snuff took early retirement.

Press activity around the High Commission was intense when Hay and Wilkins made their way back to the crime scene in the morning. They were both exhausted, having only managed a couple of hours' sleep, which only sharpened their annoyance with the mass of reporters spilling onto Grosvenor Square in front of the High Commission. The Canadians were expected soon; their flight was due at Heathrow at 7:30 AM.

Elbowing their way through the insistent throng and tersely refusing comment, they were soon inside and re-entering the official dining room. They discovered that during the early morning hours, a proper interview room had been established in a different location. Hay didn't know to what purpose this room was formally used, but the overstuffed armchairs that had been pushed to one side evoked gentlemen and brandy and cigars. Even the coffee had come up in the world, now served from a large urn in china cups bearing, Hay supposed, the Canadian coat of arms.

"They should be here soon, Wilkins?"

"Yes, sir. They're being met by Rochon and Sergeant Carpenter, the liaison officer."

Detective Sergeant Wilkins could honestly say that he loved his job. He had wanted to be a policeman since he was a small boy and had signed up at the earliest opportunity. His long-suffering girlfriend was less enthusiastic about his career choice but should have known what she was in for when she began flirting with him at that fateful dinner party three years ago.

"Mmm. Never worked with the Mounties before. Do you expect they wear those red tunics all the time?"

"Would make undercover work a sight difficult, wouldn't it?" Wilkins grinned.

"We need a good picture of this Guévin woman, Wilkins," said Hay, shifting gears. "When we're finished briefing the team, I want you to nose out whatever you can about her—hobbies, career path, the lot. Check her appointment book and search her apartment and office again. See if you can track down the ex-husband. Always a good place to start."

"Yes, sir." Wilkins paused. "But I'm not quite clear on what we're to do and what the Canadians are to do. I mean, aren't they the ones who will want to be following up on Guévin? Surely they're starting with more information on her anyway."

"You're right," acknowledged Hay. "It's a bit complicated. In fact, I spoke with the super on that score last night. Problem is, there's not a lot of precedent in a case like this. I expect we'll all have to muddle through, try not to make any waves, and let them think they're in charge. There is a unit of Special Branch equipped to deal with crimes against or threats to diplomats, but they've told the chief they only want to be kept fully informed. They'll keep their noses out for the time being."

Or their noses clean, perhaps, he thought. He didn't much like the smell of this case so far, either. Hay could tell that the super was jumpy about CID involvement on High Commission property. He had suggested that Hay tread lightly and "not rattle any skeletons," whatever that might mean. Hay was uncomfortable as well but told himself that solid, honest police work should offend no one. Police work had, in fact, been his life for some twenty-eight years now; in many ways it had precluded him from having any other. Being force-fed by his brother's wife once a fortnight was not the sum total of his social life these days, but he had to admit it was close.

"Anyway, try to get a clear picture of Guévin. Involve the Canadians. Perhaps Sergeant Carpenter, or one of the lads arriving today."

Wilkins nodded, rubbing a hand over his prematurely balding head. He sometimes thought that his boss, while no oil painting, had all the luck in the hair department.

Mary Kellick awoke abruptly at 7:23 AM, consumed by horror. Her thighs felt paralyzed, nailed to the bed, and her mouth was bone-dry. The sensation was familiar. It had been a nightmare. She was being chased by three men around and around in a circle. She kept slipping on the blood, and they kept after her. Still overwhelmed by fear, she thought she had overslept and would be late for work. But no, a policeman had told her not to report today because . . . because . . . oh God, there had been so much blood.

Three newcomers, along with the Deputy High Commissioner and Sergeant Carpenter, were ushered into what Hay already considered the Brandy and Cigars room. Hay was annoyed by his own surprise that the Canadian inspector was female: a fine-featured woman who looked like she had spent the night on a plane. Hay thought abstractedly that she must be at the bottom end of height requirements for the RCMP, whatever they were. Inspector Elizabeth Forsyth was flanked by RCMP Sergeant Gilles Ouellette and a security man from the Canadian Department of Foreign Affairs, Gerry Middleton. Hay and Wilkins briefed the team on events to date.

Liz Forsyth was attempting to concentrate but she was damnably tired. She had put in a demanding week back in Ottawa and then been summarily instructed to get to London ASAP. Looked like an interesting case, though. She knew little of Embassies and the like, and even less of the workings of Scotland Yard. It was small comfort, but the Brits looked as exhausted as her own team was jet-lagged.

She massaged her temples through a mass of untidy brown hair and tried to concentrate on the debriefing.

Liz didn't much care for international travel anymore. Suddenly she started. "This Kellick woman—you say she claimed she couldn't identify the body. Yet Sergeant Carpenter and that other fellow, the security guard—did you say McFaddon?—were both able to provide a positive ID? She's the engagements secretary, isn't she? That doesn't make any sense."

Hay raised his eyebrows. "You're right. She should be interviewed again." He refrained from suggesting *who* should conduct the interview, learning quickly about the world of diplomacy. "This is the layout," continued Hay, producing a diagram that had been provided by one of the High Commission security guards. "High Commission and Official Residence are adjoining, with internal access. Seems the High Commission offices are called the 'chancery.' Some household staff live on the premises, and there are two apartments for diplomatic staff on the top level, currently vacant due to renovations. Mary Kellick has an adjoining flat. On to forensics?"

Liz nodded. Clubbed from behind and throat slashed. *So you suspect foul play, then*, she thought irreverently but kept her mouth shut. She had learned long ago that not everyone shared her sense of humor. God, she was tired.

They worked out a plan of action whereby Hay and Forsyth would interview the program heads, as well as the High Commissioner and his wife upon their arrival. Detective Sergeant Wilkins and Sergeant Ouellette, along with security man Middleton (who immediately struck Hay as an arrogant snob), would organize the more junior members of what the Canadians were calling the "task force" into interview and investigative units to deal, initially, with the rest of the High Commission staff. Then they would turn their attention to finding out more about Guévin. Sergeant Carpenter from the High Commission would be drafted to take notes during the first interviews.

The program head interviews would begin immediately. Hay stifled a yawn. *Perhaps*, thought Liz Forsyth, the throbbing of the aircraft still in her ears, *when this series of interviews is over we can all get some sleep.*

High Commissioner Wesley Carruthers and his wife, Sharon, had gotten on the first morning flight out of Edinburgh. Carruthers had spoken several times by phone with Paul Rochon and was more or less abreast of the situation unfolding in London. Carruthers's handsome face was ashen; he was shaken and worried. His stint as "Your Excellency" had been going quite well up to this point.

Sharon Carruthers, however, was enjoying herself immensely, despite having had her little vacation cut short. She took another bite of a well-buttered croissant and chewed on it thoughtfully. She crossed her elegant legs, albeit with some difficulty as they were traveling in economy. Then Sharon turned her black-fringed cat eyes on her husband. "Isn't this *interesting*?" she wondered aloud. "Will you tell them, do you think?"

Carruthers's voice was full of misery. "I really don't know." He paused. "Will you?"

Sharon leaned her head back on her headrest and gazed at the Fasten Seatbelt light. "I'm not sure. I guess that depends on a lot of things," she mused. "Like how much they already know."

The head of the High Commission's political section resembled some sort of rodent, although no one would have mentioned it aloud. He was a spare, hungry-looking man with protruding teeth and a retreating hairline. Having grown up near the Rocky Mountains, Liz had once found rodents cute. Not this one, though. He had small, close-set, gray eyes that shifted rapidly between her and Hay.

She began, "So, Mr. . . . er"—she consulted her notes—"Jarvis."

"Harry, please," he interjected smoothly. He would doubtless have flourished his cap had he been wearing one.

"You are the head of the political section, yes?"

"The program manager, that's right. I also supervise the public affairs program."

"Tell us about your whereabouts last night, Mr. Jarvis."

"I attended a reception at the Russian Embassy from six until eight. The High Commissioner is away, and Paul—Rochon that is, the Deputy HiCom—told me he didn't feel up to another function this week. I ended up with the invitation. That kind of thing happens a lot at missions, you know," he added helpfully.

"And what time did you leave for the reception?"

"About 5:45. The Russians expect you to be on time. Not like the Euros," he mused, then realized he was being irrelevant. "I left direct from the High Commission. My wife didn't want to go. She had a headache."

I'll bet, thought Liz. She continued, "And you left . . . ?"

"Not before eight. I was having a very interesting chat with my opposite number at the Spanish Embassy. I can give you his name if you like." He gave Liz a toothy smile.

"Later, perhaps. How well did you know the victim?"

"Poor Natalie. I couldn't believe it this morning when Paul called. He was telling everyone not to come in to work until informed otherwise."

"And how well did you know her, Mr. Jarvis?"

Jarvis shifted around on his chair. "Not well. A bit. I mean, I've known her a long time in various assignments."

"And you liked her?" interjected Hay.

"Well, no, not really," answered Jarvis slowly. "It was no secret," he added defensively.

"Why did you not like Ms. Guévin?"

"Oh, just bureaucratic crap mostly."

"Meaning . . ." pursued Liz.

"She screwed me around a few years back. She was the trade participant on a promotion board when I was up for promotion. I really needed the money—our salaries have been frozen for years—and God knows I'd waited my turn. I didn't get the promotion. I learned later that she had put the knife in"—at this his eyes narrowed—"and that one of her personal fan club had been given the nod instead. After that, to make matters worse, I landed the worst posting of my life, a place I would never have been assigned had I been promoted. It was a nightmare, professionally and personally, and it's taken me a long time to recover."

Sergeant Carpenter was writing as fast as he could, but Jarvis was now speaking very rapidly. This note-taking wasn't as easy as it looked. Some days he wished he were back in the field, working for narcotics branch. Now *that* had been interesting . . . He was jolted back to his notes as Jarvis continued, "And then I land this place—I've always wanted a posting in London—and who turns up but good old Natalie Guévin. Can't tell you how pleased I was. But," he added, "I never, ever would have hurt her—or anyone else for that matter. But I figured I'd better tell you the whole story up front. As I said, it's no secret I didn't like her."

Jarvis told a convincing story, but clearly he knew how to carry a grudge. The alibi was good—one of those almost too good to be true. The timing of the reception coincided perfectly with the time of death, which was not yet public knowledge. Liz Forsyth and Stephen Hay swapped impressions following the interview. They agreed that Jarvis bore watching, and that the alibi would have to be followed up. In one important respect Hay had reached almost the same conclusion as Liz had: he thought Jarvis resembled a rabbit.

Anthony Thistlethwaite waited impatiently in the arrivals hall. The High Commissioner had called early, asking for a driver to meet their flight, and Anthony had decided to do the run himself. He had been waiting for twenty minutes already and decided to buy a paper. TRADE ENVOY BUTCHERED! roared the headline, above a picture of Natalie Guévin during last month's Canada Trade Fair. Anthony was amazed at the speed with which the story had made the papers. A highly speculative account followed, and Anthony turned his attention back to the photo. It certainly didn't do Natalie justice: women needed makeup to turn out well in black and white, and Natalie never wore any. But she had been a pretty woman, even if she was "past the first bloom of youth," as his mother would have said.

"There you are, Anthony." The quiet tones of the High Commissioner startled him, and for some reason he felt obliged to shove the paper under his jacket. "Thank you for coming out so early. Especially under the circumstances."

"It's due to t' circumstances I'm here, sir. Where is Madame?"

Madame appeared suddenly, silky black hair swinging about her shoulders. A powerful odor of expensive French perfume accompanied her. "What's the holdup?" she asked impatiently. "Let's get the hell out of here."

"Who on earth," asked Inspector Liz Forsyth, "is that strange-looking woman?"

Annie Mallett was being gently shooed out of the dining room for the fourth time that morning. Annie believed the policemen were making a mess, and she was trying unsuccessfully to enter with her feather duster and rags. Besides, she had decided that Detective Chief Inspector Hay, despite his shortcomings, did have rather nice eyes. In fact, Annie believed that he fancied her, and if only he could catch sight of her in her short blue dress, he might take the time to interview her again.

"That," sighed Hay, "is one Annie Mallett. Housemaid extraordinaire and full-time snoop. The lads can't get rid of her."

"I do believe she's winking at you." Liz grinned.

Hay grimaced. He was well aware that police work sometimes attracted a particularly ghoulish kind of groupie. He was pleased to change the subject.

"We didn't learn much from the program manager for immigration," he commented. The immigration program head, a tiny woman sporting huge glasses, had not had much to offer. "A bit of a bluestocking. She didn't have a bad word for anybody. Unless they're all just terribly discreet in that profession. And she doesn't seem to have known Guévin very well at all."

Liz wasn't entirely sure what "bluestocking" meant but wasn't about to admit it, so remarked, "Well, she said she'd only been here, what, three or four months? Following an assignment in Warsaw. So that's quite plausible. Let's hope we get more out of Lahaie."

As if on cue, Colonel Claude Lahaie, Canadian military attaché to the High Commission, strode into the room. He cut an impressive figure, standing well over six feet, with that easy yet commanding military presence. Lahaie had a strong face and a disarmingly genial manner. He was attired in full military kit. He could have "dressed down" today—it being Friday—but he felt that whenever he was on duty, especially in a foreign country, he was obliged to keep up appearances. He slid gracefully into the chair offered him and declined coffee.

"Of course I know what this is about," began Lahaie in lightly accented English. "A dreadful business. Natalie was a lovely woman."

"You knew her well?"

"Natalie wasn't one to talk about herself. She was a very private person, quiet, dedicated to her job. Couldn't abide pretense. She was a straight shooter but didn't give much of herself away. So no, I didn't know her *well*, but I liked and admired her very much."

"I understand," said Liz Forsyth, "that you were riding companions?"

Lahaie raised his eyebrows slightly. "Yes, we were."

"And you rode together often?"

"About once a week. But we talked mostly about horses. There was nothing going on, if that's what you're getting at."

"I didn't mean to suggest, sir . . ."

"No, but someone will suggest it for you. Posts are hotbeds of gossip—much of it without foundation. You might want to remember that." Lahaie smiled. "My wife always found it quite funny. She likes—liked—Natalie a lot and found the rumors quite entertaining. Anyway, we were, as you say, riding companions. Natalie and I were the only serious riders in the office. She was very good, loved the animals. But when we were together our conversation was almost exclusively about the sport."

"Do you know if she had any enemies?"

Lahaie looked steadily ahead. "Not personal ones, if that's what you mean. But she had been receiving . . . threats."

"Threats?"

Lahaie nodded. "From one of those environmentalist organizations. As you know," he addressed this to Hay, "there are many in this country who choose to become excited about sealing in Canada. Load of hogwash if you ask me. If seals looked like snakes no one would give a damn. Eighty-five percent of them are shot, anyway, not clubbed. But this post has always been an especial target for such activists, and the trade position in particular usually takes the heat."

"And Natalie Guévin was a target?" asked Hay, his heart sinking fast. He had half-believed, half-hoped this to be an internal High Commission crime, preferably committed by a Canadian. The last thing he needed was some dreadful political fiasco.

"Not at first. The issue has lost importance in recent years. Only lately has it made the newspapers again. And recently there were letters, ugly letters. Three of them aimed at Natalie directly. They were a bit—what's the word?— corny, though."

"How so?"

"They were of the style popular in crime fiction—you know, letters cut out of magazines and pasted to a page."

"Where are they now?" asked Liz.

"I don't know. In Natalie's files, I expect. She might have thrown them out. She believed they were sent by some crank, and asked me not to make a fuss. Nevertheless, she did inform all High Commission security personnel and reported the matter back to Ottawa."

"Where were you last night, Colonel?" asked Hay abruptly.

"I left the office about six o'clock. I had a few errands to run on Oxford Street. Dry cleaning, that sort of thing. I stopped for a drink at a pub around the corner. As my wife is back in Canada for a holiday, I had dinner at a tandoori place. *Not* one of the best, I'm afraid. Anyway, I was reading a book at the time and stayed at the restaurant longer than

I'd expected to. I think that I left at about nine and went home on the tube."

"How long have you been at the High Commission?" asked Liz.

"Three years."

"And prior to that?"

"I spent eighteen months in Bosnia. Before that, Somalia. This has been a nice change of pace."

As the interview was winding down, Inspector Forsyth unexpectedly asked the colonel if he would take her riding in Hyde Park the next morning. The colonel graciously acquiesced, and they made the date.

"I suppose women might find him attractive, but I didn't think he was quite *that* attractive," commented Hay afterward. "Or are all you Mounties simply that horse-mad?"

Liz was chewing her pencil. "Just an idea. Anyway, I've always wanted to ride in Hyde Park." She looked ruefully at the gnawed pencil end and asked, "Anywhere around here I can have a cigarette?"

So it had come to this. One of the finest chefs in England reduced to making sandwiches for policemen. Luciano Alfredo Carillo cleaved a large lobster open in high dudgeon. And the high-handed fashion in which Mrs. Bloody High Commissioner had spoken to him! He was treated like a flaming short-order cook in this place. *He* was alright, the High Commissioner, but then he rarely dealt with the kitchen. But *her*—a hard-faced cow if he'd ever met one. She was a lot younger than the boss, that was for sure. And very beautiful—seductive even. The chef, himself a handsome man with jet-black hair, an aquiline nose, and an admirable waistline given his profession, had even initially been somewhat attracted to Mrs. Carruthers when she first arrived at the High Commission, and had flattered himself that the attraction was mutual. But that was before the first dinner party that the Carrutherses had hosted. The chef thought it had gone perfectly well, and was most satisfied with the dinner that his kitchen had produced. Except that when it was over, Madame had barged into the kitchen and begun banging on about tough squid (it wasn't), underdone steak (it was done to a perfect medium rare), and undercooked chocolate tart (it was a lava cake for God's sake). This harangue was carried out in front of the kitchen staff and the hired waiters and without any regard for the chef's status, much less his feelings. From that day forward, a fierce hatred had burned in Carillo for the Bitch from Toronto, as he privately thought of her. Even now, at the recollection of that dreadful evening, his face began to resemble the color of the shellfish he was ruthlessly tearing to pieces.

And now she had asked—no, *told*—him to make sandwiches for the whole bleeding police force. Had he been reduced to cooking in a police canteen? Well these would be sandwiches unlike any they had ever tasted before. He had his pride and a reputation to uphold. He would start with the fresh lobster and house mayonnaise. The small cadre of kitchen staff kept their heads down and got on with their work. They were much more frightened of Carillo than of any unknown murderer.

Sharon Carruthers, wife of the Canadian High Commissioner to the United Kingdom of Great Britain and Northern Ireland, settled into her seat across from Hay and Forsyth. She leaned back comfortably into the chair, her elbows on the armrests, tilted her head, and lightly stroked the right side of her face. She smiled faintly at the investigators, smoothing her fitted skirt. She had no reason to be nervous. This was, after all, her house.

What a beautiful woman, thought Stephen Hay.

What a piece of kit, thought Liz Forsyth.

"Well, gentlemen," began Sharon Carruthers with a nod to Hay and Carpenter, "and lady." Liz managed a thin smile. The jet lag was rendering this expensively attired woman all the more irksome. "It appears that my husband and I were away during a *most* exciting time. We were in Edinburgh, you see, supposedly for a week's vacation. It was well deserved, I can tell *you*. You wouldn't *believe* the pace that Wesley and I maintain to get through all the work here at the post. And then there's the social side—positively *killing*. But we enjoy it, of course. Would you care for a coffee?"

"Er, no, thank you," said Hay, mildly confused. It was

usually his side of the table that asked that question. "How well did you know the deceased?"

"Well enough."

Hay raised a quizzical brow.

Mrs. Carruthers continued, "Well, Natalie came here shortly after Wesley and I arrived. She was, I suppose, a good enough officer. The commercial delegations seemed to like her."

"Mrs. Carruthers," said Liz, "can you tell us a bit about Natalie's social life? Friends, hobbies, that sort of thing?"

Sharon Carruthers smiled gently to herself. "Oh, that," she said. "Well, it seems she liked horses. Then again, they say so did Catherine the Great."

There was an uncomfortable silence. Liz watched Mrs. Carruthers carefully. "And what else?"

"Well, my dear," said Mrs. Carruthers, "you will find out sooner or later, won't you? She was something of a—well, there's no polite way of putting this—a, well, something of a—slut." Mrs. Carruthers looked downward as she said the last. Hay and Forsyth exchanged a look. They hadn't heard this before.

"Oh yes," continued Sharon Carruthers, leaning forward, elbows on the table. Her large green eyes were fixed on Hay, although Liz had put the question. "Yes, indeed. The number of stories I've heard about *her*. Would make your *hair* curl, my dear. Thoroughly unreliable."

Then what, thought Liz Forsyth, *was she doing in a*

highly sensitive job in the High Commission? This makes
no sense.

The interview continued for a time, and at last Hay said, "We would like to see the High Commissioner first thing this afternoon, please, if you would be so kind as to relay the message."

"Certainly. But I don't know what he can tell you that he hasn't already told Mr. Middleton."

Hay and Forsyth looked at each other in surprise. "Middleton?" asked Hay. "Gerry Middleton? He has seen the High Commissioner?"

"Yes, of course," answered Sharon Carruthers, straightening her tailored pinstriped jacket as she prepared to go. "They were together before I came across. I assumed that since he was with Foreign Affairs security he'd been detailed to question Wesley. Oh well, it will all come out in the wash no doubt. It's been a pleasure." With that and a toss of gleaming black hair she was gone.

Hay dismissed Carpenter. He sat quietly for a moment, staring down at the table and forgetting all about diplomacy and the rattling of skeletons. Then he turned slowly to Liz and asked through clenched teeth, "What the hell is this? Are you people playing a double game here? I'm not about to be cut out of my own investigation."

"Oh, it's your investigation now, is it?" asked Liz, a bit shrilly. "Ottawa will find that very interesting. And I have no idea what Middleton is up to," she said, although she sorely wished she did. "I thought he was with your boy." She looked exhausted and genuinely confused.

"So did I," said Hay, rather more gently. "I'm sorry. There must be a reasonable explanation for this. We're both bloody tired and getting snappy. Why don't we see if there's any lunch?"

"Good plan," said Liz with a nod. "Lead on."

They were only partway through an exceptional lunch of watercress soup and a delectable assortment of sandwiches when Mary Kellick pushed her way past Constable Brent, who was manning the main dining room entrance, and burst into the Brandy and Cigars room.

"I'm sorry, I'm sorry," she cried, "but I must talk to you. Must talk to you now. I'm so sorry—lunch too, sorry—but I have to see you. You see, I know. Well, not before, I didn't. I wasn't lying," she said nervously, looking from Hay to Forsyth and back again, "I just couldn't . . . tell." At this, she burst into tears, noisily sucking in gulps of air when she did come up for breath. Liz sat the hysterical woman down gently at the table and pushed a glass of ice water in front of her.

Liz had not seen Mary Kellick before. Kellick was probably only in her mid-thirties, but she looked a good deal older, especially with her face crumpled in grief. She had spoken with difficulty and was hyperventilating badly. Liz wondered if they might need to call a doctor.

Kellick was tall and almost skeletally thin. Her hair was pulled back from her face, the premature gray of the roots changing to pale blond a couple of inches from the hairline. She was dressed in a pair of plain black pants and a black sweater. Hay wondered vaguely if she was in mourning for Natalie Guévin.

"Have some water, Miss Kellick," said Hay softly. "Now, what is it that you want to tell us?"

With great difficulty, Mary steadied her voice. "Yesterday"—she turned glazed eyes to Hay—"I told you that I couldn't identify the body. I couldn't. Honestly I couldn't. But later I realized it had to be Natalie. Her hair. No one else has hair like that. But with all the . . . blood." She whispered the last word. "I'm so sorry. So very sorry."

Liz watched the distraught woman closely. "You must have liked her very much," she said.

"Oh, I did," cried Mary, looking at Liz with wide eyes. "I didn't know her well, but I did know her. She was a clever, friendly woman, you know. She was very nice to me. Not all of them are. I don't fit, you understand. They are Canadian diplomats. Then there are the local British staff. I'm a Canadian, but I've lived in England for the last twenty years, so I'm local staff too. So you see, I don't really fit."

Liz didn't see, not really, but she nodded understandingly and said, "Go on."

"Well anyway, Natalie was always nice to me. And like I said, I liked her. And when I saw that . . . that . . . thing in the anteroom, to me it *wasn't* Natalie. Not Natalie. It was something else. I didn't know what, but it wasn't her. Can you understand?"

Hay felt an unexpected jolt of very old pain. He knew exactly what she meant. Almost twenty years ago, following the accident, he had been asked to identify the body of his wife. But it hadn't been Paula. It hadn't really been the smart, funny woman he had loved beyond reason. It had been something else—something pale and waxen and expressionless. He understood Mary Kellick perfectly.

"Don't worry, Miss Kellick," said Hay gently. "We were able to identify the body. That's all that matters."

Liz shot him a sideways look. "There's one other thing, Miss Kellick," she began.

"Yes?" asked the woman, tilting her head.

"My colleagues here told me that you were doing your rounds when you discovered the body."

"That's right," said Kellick.

"Miss Kellick, of course you know there is a security staff here at the High Commission whose job it is to ensure that everything is locked up, secure and in order, every night. Can you tell me exactly what sort of 'rounds' you were doing?"

Hay looked up with sudden interest.

"Why, I was doing *my* rounds, of course," answered Kellick.

"*Your* rounds? And what precisely are *your* rounds?"

"Well, there are certain things I need to check every night. Once someone left some classified papers in one of the anterooms; if I hadn't found them he'd have been in big trouble. Another time there was a little figurine missing from the dining room, so I reported it. None of the security guards would have noticed *that*. And I make sure the lights are turned off and the stove is off in the kitchen. Things like that."

This woman is totally neurotic, thought Liz, *but dangerous? Hard to tell.* "Thank you, Miss Kellick," she said. "And thank you for clearing up the other matter. Good-bye."

Hay watched Kellick exit the room. The woman was clearly overwrought. He turned to Liz and commented, "A lot of this could have been brought on by finding the body. It was a bloody mess. Some of my own lads were uncomfortable. And to realize she knew her, to boot."

Liz nodded. "But that relentless checking of things that have nothing to do with her is deeply weird. Like the stove. And who cares if some ornament is missing from the Residence? It wouldn't belong to her anyway, and it wouldn't be her responsibility if it went missing. So what's the big deal? Unless she's just very dedicated to her job and the High Commission."

"It is, as you say, deeply weird," said Hay with the flicker of a smile. "But speaking of stoves and such, do you think there might be any of those lobster sandwiches left?"

Sergeant Roy Carpenter was piqued. This was turning into a bad day for the liaison officer. First he had been dragooned into taking notes for Hay and Forsyth while the other sergeants were off doing real police work. He hated note-taking: he had no shorthand, and he found it difficult to keep up with the rapid tempo of the interviews. Now he was stuck at Heathrow waiting for a diplomatic shipment, and the plane was late. He would have to draft a report from his notes later in the evening. Finally, he knew that the investigators were going out for a pint tonight. After all the work he had done for them—arranging an interview room, organizing the hotel and the airport meet, even serving as note-taker—they might at least have invited him for a pint of bitter. He sighed loudly and slumped more deeply into the uncomfortable orange plastic seat.

Despite herself, Liz's jet lag had prevailed and she had fallen asleep in an overstuffed armchair patterned with yellow sunflowers on a white, stripy background. Liz needed a lot of sleep and was rarely able to get enough, what with her twenty-four-hour-a-day job, running her home, and attending to the minutiae of personal administration and the gentle demands of her dog, Rochester.

Her eyes seemed to her to be permanently red and swollen, and her head often felt as if it were stuffed with cotton wool when she awoke. She had been enjoying her sleep, could have gone on for hours, but Hay was gently shaking her awake. "The High Commissioner's on his way. Wake up, Forsyth."

"Tell the High Commissioner to get stuffed," she grumbled, trying to unglue her eyelids and slowly coming to terms with her surroundings. What the hell was she doing here anyway? She'd had a nice, quiet weekend planned with her collie cross and a couple of videos. Now her dog was languishing in a kennel near her home in Aylmer, and she was so tired she could hardly see straight. She looked up at Hay. He looked worse than she felt.

"Come along, now. We've work to do." He wished that he could nap like that. She'd been out for a good twenty minutes. He never slept well unless he was in his own bed, with a solid seven or eight hours stretched out in front of him.

They had agreed not to ask the High Commissioner about Gerry Middleton, believing the matter would best be dealt with, initially at least, on their side of the table. In the end, the interview was something of a disappointment. High Commissioner Wesley Carruthers was a charming and articulate man, but if he knew anything useful he wasn't talking. He seemed truly distressed by the murder, though his choice of language befitted a government press release. He was "shocked and saddened" by the death. He had only good things to say of Natalie Guévin, but his comments seemed to be straight from an annual appraisal report. She was "thorough," "creative," "dedicated," and possessed "exceptional organizational skills."

He had little to say about her social life; he didn't like

to get involved in the personal lives of his employees. He did understand that she rode a bit. Carruthers exhibited none of his wife's predilection for gossip and innuendo. As to motive, he had no idea who might want to kill Natalie. He was aware of the threats from the anti-sealing lobby but had agreed with Natalie that they were bunk. Finally, he was horrified that such an event should have taken place on High Commission property—he would be speaking with the minister personally later today—and he hoped that the madman would be found as soon as possible.

"He seemed," said Liz afterward, "to have genuinely liked her, and to be upset by the death. In contrast to his wife."

"She was a cold fish, alright," said Hay,

"I know the type. Blue-chip Toronto stock. 'Never-met-a-man-I-couldn't-use.' Pleased to preside over dinners she hasn't cooked and spend money she hasn't earned."

"So you'd be gratified if she committed the murder," suggested Hay.

"I should be delighted," declared Liz. "But I doubt she did. She's probably too clever for that. Anyway, she was in Scotland at the time. So was he, for that matter."

"Well, stranger things have happened; you know that as well as I. Look, why don't you get to your hotel and get some rest. I'll finish up around here, and we can all meet later for a drink and a run-through."

"Sounds great. I have just one thing to do first. And that's to have a word with Middleton."

THREE

They were to meet at the Oak and Barrel at seven. Hay had arrived there early, assuming it could be difficult to get a table on a Friday night. Wilkins joined him shortly afterward, for the same reason. It had been a prudent move. The pub was already filling up, and the small table that Hay had nabbed appeared to be the last one available. The music was just a bit too loud for him, and the decibel level of the surrounding conversations was rising. This wasn't his regular pub, the Bull's Head, with its welcome if outdated restrictions on music and television. As it was, Hay found himself distracted by a World Wrestling Federation bout being broadcast somewhere behind Wilkins's head. At least this place was close to both the High Commission and the Roxborough, where the Canadians were staying.

"Useful day?" inquired Hay, before testing his pint.

"I think so, sir," replied Wilkins. "We only finished twenty minutes ago; Ouellette, poor sod, hadn't even checked into his hotel yet. I hope his bags have arrived by now—they seem to have been left behind in Ottawa. Anyway, we did quite a lot of digging on Guévin, and we might have some interesting stuff. Ouellette's alright, you know," he added. "Good officer. A bit young, maybe, but a good head for investigation."

Hay thought the comment on youth a bit odd coming from Wilkins, who must have been all of thirty-one. He spotted the Canadians standing in the door and waved them over. Inspector Forsyth, Sergeant Ouellette, and Gerry Middleton had been squinting in the entrance, trying to get their bearings. Two more pints and a glass of red wine, and they got down to business.

"Just one item first," said Liz Forsyth, lighting a king-size cigarette. "Middleton here has something to clear up."

When Middleton began to speak, Hay realized he had not heard the security man say more than a word or two before. Middleton had a shrill, somewhat whiny voice, whose only virtue was that it could easily be heard over the music.

"I believe," Middleton began, "that my visit to the High Commissioner earlier today may have caused some misunderstanding." Wilkins and Ouellette exchanged puzzled glances. "You see," he squeaked, "I have known Wesley, personally, for years. When he was just a Member of Parliament, and I was fresh out of university, I worked for him as a researcher on the Hill. I called on him for purely personal reasons, you see. I guess I should have mentioned it before, but it didn't seem important. So that's that. No harm done."

Liz looked expectantly at Hay. She wanted this member of the Canadian team—though he hadn't been her own choice—to be in the clear. But Hay's face was impassive as he continued to regard Middleton. It was Ouellette who broke in politely, "And what year was that?"

Middleton responded, "Let's see, eighty, eighty-one. Yes, eighty-one. Seems like another life now."

"Okay, fine. Thanks," Hay said with a glance toward Liz. "Now let's get on with it." Hay and Forsyth reviewed the highlights of their interviews and the unexpected intervention of Mary Kellick. "And now, you lads," said Hay, "what have you been up to?" Hay pulled on his cigarette, conscious of a mild sinus headache hovering behind his eyes. He realized it had been there all day.

With a polite nod to Ouellette, Wilkins began recapping their activities. A search of Guévin's flat had elicited nothing of importance, and her office had been similarly devoid of interest. No death threat letters had been found.

Her appointment book for yesterday, the day of the murder, indicated an early morning staff meeting, a ten o'clock call at the Ministry of Commerce, lunch with her opposite number at the Australian High Commission, an early afternoon meeting with a Canadian telecoms representative, and a four-thirty appointment with a Dr. Julian Cox of some organization called Eco-Action. A scribbled note in the margin read "Spk Claude."

"Do you have the appointment book?" asked Forsyth.

"Yes, ma'am," nodded Wilkins.

Liz winced. "Please don't call me 'ma'am,'" she said. "Makes me feel about a hundred."

"She prefers to be called *sir*," grinned Ouellette. He was quite fond of his inspector. She was one the best, and she didn't take herself too seriously. Not like a lot of the senior types he had dealt with.

"Yes," agreed Liz, "'sir' is far more dignified. 'Ma'am' sounds like someone who runs a brothel. Okay, what's next?"

Ouellette picked up the story. "Another interesting thing—I got this from Ottawa earlier today—Guévin was her married name. Her birth name was, in fact, Natalia Lukjovic. She was born in the former Yugoslavia, in a small town outside Pale. Her parents got out in the late fifties; Natalia would have been three or four. Ended up in Montreal, where her father opened up a dry-cleaning business. She was an only child and subsequently attended Université Laval. Married a Philippe Guévin in 1974. The marriage only lasted a couple of years, but she hung on to her married name and seems to have made the transition from 'Natalia' to 'Natalie.' No kids. Monsieur Guévin is now an architect in the Montreal area, and preliminary inquiries suggest he hasn't been outside Québec for at least six months. It seems they haven't been in touch for years."

Wilkins added, "Her only real hobby seems to have been the horses. Competitions, even. Seems to have done quite well in local horse shows—dressage, is it called? She joined the Canadian foreign service in 1979 and had a steady if unspectacular climb through the ranks. Postings to Buenos Aires, Singapore, Rome, Bangkok, and London."

"Nice for some," muttered Middleton into his beer.

"Not so nice for her, was it?" snapped Hay. He turned back to Wilkins, trying to ignore the strongman competition now taking place over the detective sergeant's shoulder. "Good. Is there anything further from forensics?"

"They've confirmed their preliminary findings. No evidence of alcohol, drugs, or toxins in the blood, although further tests will be run. That thing the killer used to clobber her with, the red and white club, was identified as an ax handle. Moreover," Wilkins added, "it appears that Ms. Guévin was about twelve weeks pregnant."

Liz sat on the end of the bed in her hotel room, staring blankly. Three glasses of wine had done nothing to organize her thoughts, but she doubted things would be any clearer were she stone cold sober. This was unlikely to be cleared up in a day or two. Who had killed this woman? And who had this woman been? A kind, gentle person who took the time to talk to the Mary Kellicks of the world? A promiscuous tart? A horsewoman dedicated to her job, with a quiet, even non-existent, social life?

The room was lovely, peaceful. Dark, rich paneling throughout, with heavy floral curtains sealing out the wind and drizzle. What *had* been evident was that Detective Chief Inspector Stephen Hay had not believed a word Gerry Middleton had said. A pretty shaded floor lamp illuminated a broad, deep-seated wing chair; an antique desk stood below an ornate gilt mirror. The mirror, Liz decided, she could have done without. Her eyes, rimmed in black like a raccoon's, stared back at her, and the unwelcome lines in her face were yet more deeply etched due to fatigue. Her last thought before she went to sleep was, *At least I'm going riding tomorrow.* It was a thought that had brought her comfort since she was a little girl.

It was 11:30 at night, and Mary Kellick was making meatballs. Mary loved to cook. She couldn't cook like Luciano, of course, but then he was a real *chef de cuisine*. He was nice, though, and would talk to her about cooking anytime she wanted. Mary cooked with great precision. If a recipe called for half a cup of water, she could spend up to five minutes crouching at the counter, pouring water out and adding it again until the measuring cup registered exactly half full.

Tonight's recipe included beef, veal, *and* pork, plus eggs, onions, parsley, paprika, and Worcestershire sauce. Now Mary was rolling perfect little spheres between the palms of her hands and placing them on cookie sheets.

She was, she thought proudly, a perfectionist. Not just in cooking either; she tried very hard to do things right. But that muddle over the invitations that time—she cringed yet again over the incident. She had been over it countless times in her mind, and she still didn't know what had gone wrong. How had she gotten the dates wrong? It was impossible. Surely she had checked and double-checked. Mary tried to push the unwelcome thoughts out of her head as she plunged her hands again into the bowl of wet, sticky meat.

FOUR

The stable yard was of another era—charming, right down to the cobblestones. Liz estimated that it housed some twenty to twenty-five horses, but she couldn't begin to guess at the vintage of the yard itself. She looked at the sky, realizing it was only a matter of time until the rain resumed. The penetrating damp was unpleasant. But it would be comfortable enough to ride.

Colonel Lahaie was more casually attired now, but there was no question as to his profession. Even in riding breeches and ribbed sweater, he looked every inch both officer and gentleman. He introduced Liz to the resident riding instructor, a grizzled Lancastrian with the unsurprising name of Albert Taylor. Taylor was leading a tall slate gray gelding that was already fully tacked up. He handed the reins to Lahaie.

"I were shocked to 'ear about Natalie," said Albert Taylor, doffing his peaked cap. "She were a delight to 'ave 'ere. I shall miss 'er, and no doubt so will Reckless. That were 'er 'orse, th'knows," he explained to Liz. "Well, not 'er own, but she rode it all t' time just t'same. It's not an 'orse we let just anybody ride."

"Inspector Forsyth here is with the Royal Canadian Mounted Police," Lahaie broke in. "Perhaps she might exercise Reckless today?"

Liz was about to protest—it seemed indecent somehow—but Albert Taylor acquiesced immediately. "The Mounties, is it?" he said, impressed. "'Ast thou e'er seen that musical ride of theirn?"

"Sure. In fact, I was assigned to it for three years early on. Best detail I ever had." She meant it.

Now there was no question: Liz should have Reckless. She disappeared to groom and tack up the horse herself, to the surprise of the old instructor. "She's a bit like Natalie in 'er ways, int she?" he asked Lahaie. "Natalie always did that an' all."

The Anglo-Arab craned her neck around and rolled her eye to get a better look at the person who had just entered her stall. The bay mare was already spanking clean but evidently believed she merited the full treatment anyway. The tack room was in the center of the barn. Liz found the locker with Reckless's name on it and pulled out the grooming kit. She brushed the mare's glossy coat and picked out her already pristine hooves, but at least Reckless seemed mollified.

Liz returned to the locker to fetch the bridle and fine English-made saddle. She slung the saddle over her forearm and grabbed the headpiece of the bridle with her other hand. Suddenly she froze and hurriedly replaced the tack. In the back of the locker was a small pile of riding clothes. "Plain view," she muttered to herself, inwardly rehearsing the exceptions by which police officers could obtain evidence without a warrant. She carefully riffled through the clothing. There was one unexpected find. A note, computer-generated and printed on good-quality bond, had evidently been wadded tightly into a ball and then smoothed out again to be placed carefully under a pair of tan riding breeches. Liz didn't have a plastic bag on her, although some were in her purse in front of Reckless's stall. She couldn't risk running back and confronting Lahaie or Taylor, so she hastily folded the piece of paper and stuffed it in her jodhpurs. Liz then quickly tacked up the mare, who had become quite indignant with waiting.

DCI Hay was on his third cup of coffee and his fifth cigarette. The Saturday papers had already been dissected and were scattered across the dining room table. He had another hour or so before he needed to get to the High Commission given his new colleague would still, no doubt, be trampling the flowers in Hyde Park.

Not a brilliant day for a ride, he thought as he looked out the window at the gathering clouds. He wandered into the kitchen to refill his cup and leaned back against the kitchen counter. He still liked this house. It was an attractive two-story in Pimlico, inherited from his father some ten years ago. The house could be a bit cranky—especially the plumbing—but it had been a good home despite its vintage. It was, in fact, the house of a man who lived alone and was comfortable with it. It was decorated to his taste: not overfurnished, but with furniture of good quality. Some of it might have been antique, although Hay just thought of it as old. A few nice oils, a good mantel clock, the occasional piece of pottery, and several hundred books—largely French and English literature.

It was not a house that had seen a woman's influence; there was an absence of dried flowers, ornaments of any kind were infrequent, and the requirement for a complete dinner service had never been foreseen. Since losing Paula those many years ago, Hay had chosen to live alone and had never seen any reason to do otherwise. There had been others since, of course, but he had never again experienced the intensity of passion he'd had for Paula, and anything less was, quite simply, not good enough. This house suited

Hay. He supposed he would be there a long time yet.

He remained leaning against the counter, gazing out the window at his small garden. He was still vexed about this Middleton business. He thoroughly disliked the squeaky Canadian security man, although he was not entirely sure why. Lighting another cigarette, Hay wondered whether Middleton's story would stand up under closer scrutiny. And if it would be undiplomatic for him to make a few independent inquiries.

He didn't know if Middleton was lying, but it would be unsurprising. Hay had been lied to many times in his life; he was a policeman after all. When he thought about it, it seemed that most of the people he dealt with on the job lied about something or other. Any piece of information could be denied, distorted, or embellished. Sometimes people lied to cover up a crime, but more often than not lies were simply designed to obscure unworthy actions, indiscretions, or character flaws. Lies were expected.

When they came from colleagues or people he cared about, however, Hay was less philosophical. These were not lies—this was betrayal. And he had been betrayed too many times. As a young constable he had learned that a so-called friend was belittling him behind his back while pretending to be best mates. And then a boss whom he had tried very hard to please had used him as a dumping ground for unfinished work simply because he knew that the conscientious Hay would do it, and do it well. And then Sarah, a lady he once believed he would marry, betrayed him in the way that only a woman can.

Yes, it had made him bitter, not that he would have used that word. He retained enough faith in people—not suspects, of course, but regular people—to give them the benefit of the doubt, for a while at least. *Five minutes anyway.* When faith proved justified, he was as loyal a friend or lover as any. But if it did not, he turned away and never looked back. Hay remembered imperfectly a quotation from *Pride and Prejudice*, from Darcy, to the effect that his good opinion once lost was lost forever. He knew that this had come back to mock Darcy, but it was a damn good motto nonetheless.

Hay knew that he had become increasingly suspicious over the years, and inclined toward waspishness. He was happy enough to carry a grudge and felt no compulsion to apologize for it. He had become angrier, too, in recent years. Less able to suffer fools at all, let alone gladly, and his definition of fools had become wider. He was saddened by this but seemed incapable of reversing it. And perhaps, he thought, he didn't want to; perhaps it was time he grew up.

Dr. Julian Cox, co-founder of Eco-Action, ushered Ouellette and Wilkins into the sitting room of his cluttered apartment. "I suppose I've been expecting you," he said, once settled into the depths of his armchair.

The apartment didn't look as though it was expecting

anyone. Newspapers, books, and magazines littered every surface, and papers were heaped haphazardly on the floors. One wall was stacked almost to the ceiling with yellowing documents, and there was an unpleasant odor, both sour and sweet, in the room. Amid the disorder, a few struggling houseplants vied for sunlight. A tabby cat leaped from a pile of newsprint onto the arm of Cox's chair and stared balefully at the visitors. Wilkins hoped that his allergies wouldn't flare up. He didn't like cats anyway, found them somewhat sinister and disconcertingly boneless.

Another wall made a convenient bulletin board to which posters, pamphlets, and bulletins were carelessly affixed with great swathes of masking tape. A baby seal, eyes black and suffering, stared silently at the newcomers from an anti-sealing poster. SAVE THE PLANIT!! exclaimed a great green-and-black banner strung across one of the longer walls.

"My daughter," explained Cox, following Ouellette's gaze. "She was only five when she did that. Lives with her mother now, of course."

"Why were you expecting us, sir?" asked Wilkins.

"It's in all the papers, isn't it? And I saw Natalie Guévin Thursday afternoon. Stands to reason. Care for a coffee?"

Wilkins shook his head, stifling a grimace. "What did you want to see Miss Guévin about, Dr. Cox?"

Cox tapped his pipe against the heel of his boot. "I didn't."

"You didn't?"

"Nope, she asked to see me. She was quite angry, actually. It was about an Internet site, one affiliated with us. There's an 'Enemies of the Environment' page, and someone had added Natalie's mug shot to it. I didn't have anything to do with that, although I didn't necessarily disagree with the choice. It's this bloody sealing business in Canada, you see," said Cox, the pitch of his voice changing a bit. "A disgraceful, inhumane slaughter. The Canucks seem to want to ignore the carnage, babbling on about traditional rights and depletion of the cod stocks—hypocritical nonsense, of course. Anyway, Natalie had stumbled across the Internet site, or at least someone had told her about it, and she was livid."

"So you had an argument."

"No, actually, we didn't. I agreed to try to have her deleted from the page, even though it wasn't on our own website. She was fine with that. Then we had something of a discussion of the issues. Climate change, emissions, that sort of thing. I'd always found her quite well informed—even liked her in a way."

"You had known her for long?" asked Ouellette.

"Since she came to London. I make a point of getting to know the relevant Embassy officials."

"And your relationship had always been good?"

"Of course not." Cox smiled. "We often came to blows over the sealing. And leghold traps. It could hardly have been otherwise. Things became quite . . . heated during our anti-sealing demonstration at the Canada Trade Fair last month, in fact." He smiled at the memory. That had been a good day. "But then she always took a harder line than Wesley."

"You are referring to the High Commissioner?" asked Ouellette. "You know him too?"

A telephone rang from somewhere amid the papers, but Cox waved it off vaguely. "Oh yes. We first met awhile back, at the Environment Conference in Rio. All the bigwigs were there, yakking up a storm. Talk about gas emissions." He smiled at his joke. "Anyway, Wesley was Canada's environment minister at the time."

"At what time did you leave the High Commission Thursday afternoon?" asked Wilkins.

"Do me a favor, Sergeant. You know very well it was about 5:15. The High Commission log must have told you that." The phone rang again. "Answering service'll get it," grumbled Cox, who seemed to be enjoying the interview.

"What did you do afterward?"

"I came home and went on to a six o'clock meeting with colleagues. We're organizing the press so that we can get some actual footage of the sealing early next year. That should get the ball rolling." He showed some yellowing teeth through his beard. "Then we went to dinner at a Vietnamese place, The Saigon."

Ouellette had been staring hard at Dr. Julian Cox

throughout the interview, trying to place that intelligent face with its abundance of facial hair. Then he got it. Dr. Cox had been one of the ringleaders of a group of anti-sealing activists who had been severely clubbed and beaten by Canadian sealers somewhere in Quebec last year. He knew he had seen that face before.

Cox closed the door slowly as the young sergeants departed. He returned thoughtfully to the sitting room and sank again into his armchair. Reflecting on the conversation with the police, he realized he should probably have expressed more sympathy for the victim, but that wasn't really his way. People were all very well, but when it came right down to it, they did much more harm than good. Look what they were doing to the environment, the wild-life, even the atmosphere.

His gaze fell upon his unfinished article, which detailed the atrocities committed by the sealers in the Canadian north. He was lucky, really, to have so much time to devote to his worthy causes. It was not as though he actually had to work, having been sole heir to a considerable fortune upon his father's unexpected passing, just as Julian was completing his latest degree at Cambridge. It must be a sign, he thought, that he was meant to devote his talents and energies to saving the planet from mankind. Or in this case, perhaps, womankind.

"And just what," Sharon Carruthers asked her husband, "am I supposed to do about that carpet?" She was carefully outlining her lips with a medium-brown pencil.

"Don't, Sharon. Please. Not now."

Sharon smiled a little and snapped shut her powder compact. "It's white, you see. Brand new white carpeting from Toronto. Must have cost a bomb. Now it's soaked straight through, all the way around. Full of blood." She shook her head. "Never knew blood was that dark a color." She wrinkled her pert surgically sculpted nose and added, "Smells nasty, too."

High Commissioner Wesley Carruthers fled his wife. Sharon gave a little shrug, refastened an insubordinate button on her cuff, and poured some more black coffee into her china cup.

Hay was wading through the forensics report. No matter how often he read these documents, he was always bemused by the unusual, if scientifically correct, use of the English language. He found himself quite comfortable in the Brandy and Cigars room, with its collection of fine hunt prints, its richly colored Azeri carpets, and the melodic wall clock with its impressive timekeeping. How long they would be allowed to stay here was another matter; the rationale for the task force remaining on the premises was rapidly fading, and they would probably be assigned back to the Yard fairly soon. At least when they did move, thought Hay, they wouldn't have to wade through oceans of reporters every morning.

He hated the press. Years ago, as a freshly minted sergeant, he had been badly misquoted by a reporter, resulting in a serious reprimand from his commanding officer. During his career he had seen many a promising young officer embarrassed, if not compromised, by genuine attempts to be informative and helpful to the press. Of course the dealings between CID and the press had now become extremely formalized and regularized. It was unlikely that any young officer might be put in a vulnerable position again, but Hay's loathing of the "gentlemen of the press" endured.

It annoyed him that there was as yet no suspect in custody. Of course it was early days, but lately he had become accustomed to cases that almost solved themselves. He often found himself wondering if the criminal classes were in fact becoming stupider.

Inspector Liz Forsyth bounded in from her morning's ride. Like a Labrador puppy, he thought ungenerously. She certainly looked better for it, though, younger even. Not so plain. What was she anyway—late thirties, early forties? Anyhow, a couple of hours on horseback with the colonel had rendered her a new woman. She probably hadn't given a moment's thought to the case, he thought, and said, a bit stiffly, "Good morning, Forsyth. You enjoyed Hyde Park?"

"Wonderful. I'll tell you something, though—Guévin must have been a fine horsewoman. That mare is quite a handful, and I'm no amateur myself. She's not at all spooky. She's bold enough but strong and a bit opinionated." Liz stopped, thinking she detected signs of boredom. "Do you ride, Hay?"

"Good Lord, no."

She shook her head, "With a name like that, too." He didn't laugh. With a little sigh, Liz sat. Like pulling teeth this morning.

Hay inquired politely, "And how is the dashing colonel today?"

"Seems alright. I've found something out, though, that could be important."

"You Canadians conducting a parallel investigation again, are you?"

Liz looked quickly at Hay and saw he wasn't joking. "Of course not." She felt her shoulders stiffen slightly. "It was just something Lahaie said yesterday that I thought might usefully be followed up. As it happened, I got the answer without the colonel's help. This is it, if you're at all interested." She slid a crumpled piece of paper in front of him.

Liz watched Hay as he read the note. Had she stepped on some toes here? It had only been a hunch, after all. Not her fault if it had paid off.

> Natalie my love,
> You're wrong, you know. And to prove it, I've
> told her. She will give me a divorce, but only

once we're all out of here; she doesn't want a public scandal. We can wait that long, surely? You must know by this how I feel. See me tonight, please. You know where.

No date, no signature. "Where did you find this?"

"In the tack locker at the stables. Underneath a pair of breeches."

"Plain View?" inquired Hay dryly.

"Plain View," replied Liz.

"If you say so," said Hay. "Did you mention it to Lahaie?"

"No. I thought if we were to follow up with him we could bring him back here for questioning."

He noticed the deliberate use of the word *we* and regarded her steadily. "So what was this famous hunch of yours?"

"Remember yesterday when Lahaie said there had been rumors about Guévin and him? He said his wife had laughed, found it amusing. I would suggest that no matter how much a woman trusts her husband, she finds nothing remotely funny about people thinking he's having an affair. At least, I never did." She flushed slightly, then continued, "Unless, of course, the wife knows for a fact that the alleged *other woman* is very seriously involved with someone else."

Hay nodded. This was all becoming very interesting.

"I had thought I would pursue the point with Lahaie. 'There is no secret so close as that between a rider and his horse,'" she declared.

Hay raised an eyebrow.

"Robert Smith Surtees," she said, then added helpfully, "1805 to 1864. But as it happened, I didn't have to raise it with him at all."

"So what did you talk about?"

"Peacekeeping, mostly."

"Peacekeeping? The topic of choice among the horsey set?"

Liz was pleased to see that the DCI had lost his earlier stiffness and was back to what she hoped was his usual self. "Quite interesting, really. Lahaie seems to be one of the few senior army officers to have managed a blemish-free service record. Quite a feat in the Canadian forces. Ever since that business in Somalia a few years back, the press has been out for blood. A Canadian soldier can't sneeze the wrong way without making the front page and sparking a formal inquiry. It's a true shame. Anyway, Lahaie seems to have maneuvered his way pretty effectively through that particular minefield."

For some reason, Hay was finding the virtues of Colonel Lahaie the tiniest bit irritating. "So he didn't actually have anything interesting to say," he observed.

"Well, if it's dirt you're after, he did say there had been some trouble in one of the sectors while he was in command. Something about allegations of impropriety by Canadian soldiers in a Bosnian hospital and rumors of black marketeering. He didn't elaborate much. He said there had, in fact, been a few disciplinary problems, but the culprits had been dealt with and sent home. It seems there wasn't much to it, and he appears to have come out of it alright."

"No doubt," grumbled Hay.

"He also mentioned that Natalie had asked him about rumors of a Western drug-trafficking operation out of Bosnia, something about drugs transiting through Bosnia from Central Asia. There were some rumors flying about that as well, and the implication was that some of the Russian and even Western peacekeepers or other agencies might be involved. But those rumors only surfaced after Lahaie's tour, and he was out of there by then."

"Of course he was," said Hay. He was starting to look bored again.

"Oh yes, one other thing. I asked him if he knew what that notation 'Spk Claude' in Guévin's appointment book might have meant. He said the only thing he could think of was that it might be connected with a horse show they planned to attend on the weekend. That she might have had a question about that."

"Mmm," said Hay, having heard enough about the colonel. "Anyway, I've a bit more information from forensics. They've catalogued a file drawer full of prints from the anteroom and the dining room. Nothing interesting at the moment, but at least we'll have them for comparison purposes if we need them. We have a bit more on Guévin as well. One of your chaps from Ottawa called for Ouellette, but he was out with Wilkins at the time interviewing the eco-tourist."

"Don't you mean *eco-terrorist*?"

"Whatever." Hay smiled for the first time that day. "Anyway, for what it's worth, that small dry-cleaning business the father started in Montreal has grown into something of an empire. He's made a lot of money out of one-hour service, it seems. Moreover, it appears that Mr. Lukjovic is something of a Serb nationalist, very active in the Canadian Serbian community. He seems to be harassing your Foreign Affairs for early release and dispatch of the body back to Montreal."

Hay paused for breath. "And that club, the one used to bludgeon Guévin. Clean of prints, by the way. It was already bagged when Sergeant Carpenter went in to ID the body, so he never had a chance to see it. But he dropped by this morning and we had a chat. When I described it to him— white ax handle tipped in red—he said it sounded a lot like what the Canadian hunters use to club seal pups."

"So you've been a busy boy. I suppose all of this is supposed to make me feel guilty about going for my ride."

"Not at all," said Hay, "you've brought back a nice little note. I think that we might spend some time now in trying to identify its author. I have a few hunches of my own."

"So have I," agreed Liz, "but first I have to call home and see how Rochester's doing."

"You have a lover called Rochester?" Hay asked, lifting an eyebrow.

"I have a mongrel dog called Rochester," she answered, choosing to ignore the other part of the question. "But you know," she continued gravely, "you really ought to try horseback riding. With your name . . ."

"Don't push your luck, Forsyth," he grumbled.

Annie Mallett had been meeting Ethel and Sybil on Saturdays for close to twenty years. They had started at The Cock and Lion but had gone off the food after that trouble with the haddock. Then The White Hart had burned down, and they settled on The Victoria and Albert. They never ran out of things to talk about. Sybil's aches and pains alone could keep them going for hours. Annie smiled to herself. Not that Sybil's problems ever stopped her going to the pub, especially not on a Saturday. Anyway, the girls would always show for what they liked to call "a good old natter."

Today, Annie was early. She knew she would be the center of attention and had dressed for the part. Today it would be Annie who had all the news because of all the exciting goings-on at the High Commission. So she was wearing her new rust-colored wool dress from M&S. Who said you had to be twenty and thin to wear a wool dress? She looked womanly, curvy. The dress Annie had carefully accessorized with the little pewter and amber brooch her Lily had sent her from America. Her hair was carefully back-combed upward in an orange—well, Annie called it auburn—flame, and she had on her tiny pearl earrings. Real pearls, mind, not artificial ones.

Of course Annie had a theory about the murder, but she wasn't about to tell the girls. She might tell that detective chief inspector, though. He would surely be impressed if she solved the case all by herself. She might be a type of Miss Marple, really. She was certainly clever enough. Though much younger, of course. Annie had become quite impressed by the DCI of late. He didn't have a pretty face, but it was strong. Full of character, she thought, although he didn't smile much. Maybe he didn't have much to smile about.

The landlord, wiping glasses as landlords are wont to do when bored, glanced over at Annie and smiled. There she was, sitting bolt upright in a dimly lit booth. These funny old birds came in every Saturday, sipping their sherry and munching their scratchings. He shouldn't laugh, really—they tipped well and didn't start fights.

"Cooo-eee!" cried Sybil from the doorway. "Hallo, luv!" called Ethel. They bustled over and squeezed in beside Annie Mallett. "Now, my dear," breathed Sybil, "tell us all about it!"

Lester Wilmot, proprietor of the Great North Furrier in East London, was about to close the store early. Trade had been a little slow today, except for that small rush of browsers about an hour ago, and Lester could afford to shut the doors and get home to Mrs. Wilmot's chicken pot pie. Lester chuckled, wondering why he and his wife had insisted on calling each other "Mr. Wilmot" and "Mrs. Wilmot" all these years. Everyone else called him Lester. He supposed it was just one of those little private jokes that married people had—a small thing in itself, yet ultimately intimate, meaningful.

The move to London two years ago was the best thing he had ever done, if you didn't count marrying Mrs. Wilmot. Almost thirty years ago, the wedding, he realized with a start. Lester didn't miss Toronto much, and they were both much happier here. Mrs. Wilmot had made some good friends and was even talking about taking out British citizenship. The thought would never have crossed their minds before, but now they were thinking seriously about it.

The move had been good for the business as well. His brother, Alex, had been happy to stay behind and run the Canadian store, and was in a position to seek out high-quality Canadian furs and ship them to the London outlet for sale. These environmentalists were a constant irritant, though. The harassment had seemingly peaked earlier in the year, but there was always a danger of the ruffians hanging about outside the store and doing their best to damage trade.

Lester closed out his cash drawer. Well, of course there was no cash; no one paid cash for fur coats. But there was a nice credit card receipt for that handsome fox jacket he had sold this morning. They really should try to get up to the Lake District this summer, he thought. Everyone had been urging them to go, but he had been unable to leave the store for that long. Now, though, he was in a position to hire some staff, and perhaps he could find someone trustworthy enough to take care of the shop while he and Mrs. Wilmot took a week's vacation. Perhaps two weeks.

Lester Wilmot gazed from behind his counter toward the display window. He could see a few Christmas lights already twinkling in the window of the high-end clothing store across the street. He must get his own decorations up on Monday, he thought with a little thrill of anticipation. Christmastime was the best part of living in London. It was like something out of Dickens, with the excited apple-cheeked children running about and Christmas carols being piped into every shop. Maybe he should have some music in his store this year as well.

He had heard nothing at all behind him. The wire was tightening around his neck in an instant. He hardly felt a thing—well, not much anyway—as his windpipe snapped in two.

FIVE

Mary Kellick didn't really mind working at home, especially on brainless, repetitious tasks like writing out invitations. There wasn't much else to do so early on a Sunday morning anyway. She sat at the kitchen table, with its French country motif, filling out invitations to the High Commissioner's annual Christmas reception. At least it would be sunny today, she thought, with that beautiful bright light already streaming into the kitchen. Mary was conscious of the faint leftover smell of onions and garlic from last night's goulash. She had, of course, thrown it out once it was cooked. She never ate anything she made—just cooked it. She never ate much of anything at all these days, really.

Sometimes when she was making a stew or putting a chicken in the oven to roast, she would imagine that a handsome, charming stranger would appear at her door. His mission was unclear: Perhaps a mutual acquaintance had suggested he call on her. Or he had seen her on the High Street and been intrigued. Anyway, her apartment would be full of wonderful, welcoming odors—rosemary, of course, and perhaps thyme and garlic—and he would stay to dinner. But this hadn't happened yet.

The last time that Mary had met a charming stranger, some years ago, it had ended badly. He was a Canadian businessman who had been on a trade mission to London, and Mary had allowed herself to be swept off her feet. She doubted that he ever learned about the baby after he went back to Canada. Not that she had been able to carry it to term anyway. Sometimes she missed the baby, though. She didn't know if it had been a boy or a girl, but she fancied that it was a girl. She had always wanted a girl.

The then High Commissioner had been very kind to her and very angry about the businessman. He had promised that she could always depend on keeping her job at the High Commission, no matter what. Mary had taken a period of stress-related leave but had never really felt the same since losing the baby those many years ago. Even now, when she saw a woman with a big baby-filled belly, she felt empty inside. Sometimes she felt angry, but mostly she just felt empty.

She selected a soft-tipped black pen for her purposes. The softer the tip, the less her hand ached from writing. She swallowed some coffee and continued with her task. The heavy, gold-embossed cards read,

> The High Commissioner of Canada and Mrs. Carruthers Request the Pleasure of the Company of (here was a blank to be filled in) for (another blank) on (blank) at (blank).

Mary filled in the blanks in her elegant, flowing script. *H.E. Mmutlane Mapandere and Mrs. Mapandere*, she wrote in the first blank. *A Christmas reception.* Mary was a little surprised. She hadn't really supposed there would be a reception this year, not under the circumstances. *Tuesday, December 16, 1997.* She had expected it would be canceled. But Mrs. Carruthers had told Mary yesterday to get on with it. She had spoken quite sharply, too, Mary thought. The Christmas reception, with its traditional tourtière and the colonel's "Moose Milk," was not, according to Mrs. Carruthers, just the most popular annual event on the diplomatic circuit. It was an obligation on the part of the High Commissioner. *7:00 to 9:00 PM*, wrote Mary.

At the bottom of the card, she drew a neat line through

the embossed letters RSVP and wrote *To Remind* overtop. All of the guests had already been invited by phone, of course—last Monday and Tuesday, recited Mary—and the cards would be sent by hand tomorrow. Mrs. Carruthers had reminded Mary pointedly that Paul Rochon must personally check all the invitations before they went. As if Mary didn't know that. It had been like that since the time she had messed up. Paul was always nice about it, though. *H.E. Maurice La Framboise and Mme. La Framboise*, wrote Mary, *a Christmas reception*.

Liz had slept extremely well; the bedcovers had hardly been disturbed and some lines from her pillow were etched into her face. Her head felt clear. She had risen early and sat for a time on the edge of the bed, watching through her window for signs of life to return to the street below. She felt content here, despite the grimness of her assignment. Liz had been born in England, in Lancashire, but hadn't been back for years. She had only been small when her family emigrated—a bit like Natalie Guévin, she realized. England hadn't left her, though; there was something in the air, or the light, or somehow in the very texture of the place that was familiar, that made her feel comfortable, at home.

She needed coffee and ordered a large pot with her breakfast. "One cup or two?" asked the room service voice. Liz smiled to herself, supposing it mustn't be all that unusual for hotel guests to invite visitors to their room and have them stay for breakfast. "Just one," she answered, then, feeling a need to explain, "I need a lot of caffeine this morning."

Liz had been alone for some time now. The trust had left her a long time ago, during the brief marriage, and she couldn't honestly say that she had given anyone a serious chance since. No time, anyway. She splashed about in the bathroom for a while, and by the time she was ready, the room service waiter was at her door with a tastefully arranged tray, single carnation in a white bubble glass vase, folded newspaper, and enormous thermos of coffee.

At 6:34 AM exactly, at least according to the hotel's digital alarm clock, three things happened simultaneously. Liz took the first bite of her breakfast, she spotted the headline on the front page of the *Times*, and the phone rang. It was Hay.

"Yes, good morning, Hay. Yes, I've just seen it," she said. "Does it relate?"

"Not necessarily," answered Hay. "But he's a Canadian, and the fur thing struck me at once of course. The MO is different, though. Even more gruesome, this one." Liz had been rapidly scanning the page, but Hay saved her the trouble. "Garroted, you see, with the ends of the wire suspending the poor bugger from two of his own coat display racks. The Yard obviously didn't see any immediate connection, or they'd have called last night."

"Can you get over here at once, Hay? Get Wilkins, and I'll muster Ouellette."

"Right away."

The thermos had only just been opened. The hollandaise sauce, so artistically drizzled over the poached eggs, had begun to congeal into tiny yellow blobs. The English muffins were rapidly becoming sodden. But Liz wasn't really all that hungry anymore.

"You see what they're doing, of course," said Sergeant Ouellette to DS Wilkins as they sped to Dr. Julian Cox's flat. "Guévin was killed in the fashion of a baby seal, right down to the ice floe."

Wilkins was driving. He'd let Ouellette drive his Escort once before and they had kept landing on the wrong side of the road. "Ice floe? What are you talking about?"

"The carpet. White. Same effect, isn't it? Blood against a white background." They entered a roundabout with surprising speed, and Ouellette pushed his foot down harder on his personal pretend brake. Why couldn't the Brits drive on the right side of the road like everyone else?

"And this one?" asked Wilkins. "Is this supposed to symbolize anything?"

"It's the way some trappers kill small animals—foxes, muskrats, that sort of thing. It's called a *collet* in French. They string up a small wire noose, usually between two trees, low to the ground. When the animal walks or runs into it, it pulls tight around the neck, garroting the animal or breaking its neck. So you see? Sound familiar? That's got to be the connection. These eco-warrior types have become eco-terrorists."

Wilkins grimaced. If trapping was that grisly maybe these environmentalists had a point. But he wasn't so sure about the connection. It was possible, of course, or Hay and Forsyth wouldn't have dispatched them to pick up Cox for further questioning. Wilkins screeched around the corner of Dr. Cox's street on two wheels. And Ouellette had thought they drove badly in Montreal.

Having sent "the lads" to bring in the Eco-Action chief, Hay and Forsyth were now standing uncomfortably on the stoop of a neat little bungalow in Wimbledon. It was a beautiful day for this time of year—sunny, crisp, and invigorating. This was a pretty home, with its fresh teal-blue paint on the window frames. A great wreath, full of dried boughs, grasses, and flowers, hung cheerily on the door. The garden flowers were gone of course, but the trees and shrubs had managed to hold on to their rich green hues. The street was very quiet, peaceful save the occasional musical intervention of a songbird.

"I'll bet you'd rather be riding," commented Hay softly and rang the bell.

"You're not kidding," whispered Liz, wishing herself anywhere except on the stoop of the lovingly maintained home of the freshly widowed Mrs. Wilmot. A middle-aged woman, dishrag in hand, slowly opened the door.

Of course they shouldn't be here at all, thought Hay. This was clearly off his patch, and he'd had a difficult time explaining to his boss why he should be conducting another interview with the grieving Mrs. Wilmot. The super had not seemed very impressed with Hay's ruminations about a connection between the High Commission murder and that of the furrier. But in the end he had been guided by Hay's hunch and had reluctantly granted permission.

"Mrs. Wilmot?" began Hay.

"Nay," the woman answered quietly, "Jenkins. Mrs. Jenkins. I'm her neighbor, poor lass."

Hay made the introductions. "May we have a word with her, please?"

"Nay," responded Mrs. Jenkins as evenly as before. "She's exhausted, poor thing. Up cryin' the whole night, wasn't she. She needs her rest now. Best thing for her."

Hay pressed on. "We really must speak with her, just for a few minutes."

Mrs. Jenkins shook her head decidedly. "That wouldn't be possible. Anyhow," she continued, "some of your lot were here last night already. Asking her a lot of questions and upsettin' her. That's enough for now, officers."

"We know, Mrs. Jenkins," tried Liz, "but it is really most important that we—"

A hoarse voice strained from somewhere inside the house. "It's alright, Millie. Tell them they can come in." Millie Jenkins twitched her head but stood back so they might enter.

Gerry Middleton, the Foreign Affairs security man, was out sightseeing on a glorious December Sunday. His work at the High Commission had wrapped up early and to his complete satisfaction. Then again, Gerry Middleton was usually satisfied with himself. He had left the police to their tedious inquiries, and surely he might profit from this unexpected visit to this "green and pleasant land." Blake. Middleton smiled. Sometimes he even impressed himself.

A product of Queen's University and holding a doctorate in political philosophy, Middleton had landed a non-rotational security position at Foreign Affairs some fifteen years ago. He was enjoying his time in the shadowy world of intelligence and was generally pleased to let anyone—colleagues, acquaintances, or his infrequent lovers—believe that he actually knew rather more than he did. He felt it gave him a certain cachet to pretend that he had just a little bit more information than did his interlocutors about any given subject. Of course, he couldn't reveal just what that information might be. Gerry Middleton would have been most surprised to know that anyone found him a pompous, insufferable bore.

The top level of the bright red double-decker tourist

bus, stopped now, was a tremendous vantage point from which to view the delights of the city. Middleton, wearing a Tilley hat to keep the sun away from his balding scalp, suddenly craned his neck a bit to get a better look. Wasn't that Colonel Lahaie, the High Commission's military attaché? And surely that was Sergeant Carpenter, the High Commission's RCMP liaison officer. What on earth were they arguing about?

"Sit down, dear." Margaret Wilmot gestured for Liz to make herself comfortable. Mrs. Wilmot was probably in her mid-sixties, petite, with white hair tied up in back. She seemed a pretty woman, but the swelling of her eyelids and the puffiness in her face were a testament to the freshness of her grief. She attempted to smile at her visitors and asked Mrs. Jenkins if she would be a dear and make tea. With Mrs. Jenkins thus occupied, Mrs. Wilmot began, "I apologize on Millie's behalf. She's a love, really. I don't know how I should have made it this far without her." Liz thought she detected a trace of a Maritime accent.

"We're terribly sorry, Mrs. Wilmot, about what's happened," said Liz. And she was, genuinely sorry, looking into Margaret Wilmot's glazed, grieving eyes. "We know the police have already been to see you, but we have a few additional questions."

Mrs. Wilmot nodded, saying only, "Yes."

"Mrs. Wilmot, prior to—the event, did you have any

reason to believe that your husband's life was in danger?" asked Liz.

As though oblivious to the question, Mrs. Wilmot began to speak, her eyes unfocused. "He was late, you see. Not so very late, but it was late for him." She smiled faintly as she mouthed the words. "And he was supposed to be coming home early, for one of his favorite dinners. Chicken pot pie." Her brow creased momentarily in some private confusion at this, then she continued, "He called to tell me he'd be a bit early. He's thoughtful like that." Her face clouded over. "Then," she said, "I called the store when he didn't turn up. It's not like him. Not like him at all." The tears began to make their way down now-familiar tracks. "Of course I tried to call several more times, and when he still didn't come home, I called the police. They went to the store, you see. Then they called me." Her voice was growing yet more hoarse.

Millie Jenkins arranged the tea things on the glass-covered coffee table and shot a murderous look at Liz Forsyth. How dare they force Margaret over all that again. They were as bad as the reporters, going into detail like that. She had thrown out this morning's paper, with its ghastly descriptions, and she would continue to rubbish the lot of them until the whole thing had blown over. Now she wished these two policemen would just leave and let Margaret get some rest. She stomped out of the sitting room.

Liz tried again. "Can you think of anyone who might

have wanted to harm your husband, Mrs. Wilmot?" she asked gently.

"No one who knew my Mr. Wilmot could have wanted to hurt him," she said. "He was a good, decent man, a wonderful husband to me. We never had kids, you see. We were everything to each other." The tears were flowing steadily, but Margaret Wilmot did her best, fumbling for a handkerchief. Hay swiftly swept a clean one from a pocket and proffered it. "The only trouble we ever had was with those environmentalists," she said, wiping at her eyes. "He doesn't even sell seal anymore, not so much as a pair of mittens. We thought that was the end of it. But then it was the leghold traps, and it all started up again."

"Did they harass your husband, Mrs. Wilmot, these environmentalists?" asked Hay. "Threaten him in any way?"

Margaret Wilmot nodded. "Twice they spray-painted horrible things on the shop window. And for a time they came to the store every week, hanging around outside and intimidating the customers."

"Intimidating them?"

"Yes, you know, telling them that only butchers and murderers bought fur. Calling them killers and threatening them. They even spray-painted one of our customers. Green paint, it was. She was wearing her brand new coat out of the store. Mr. Wilmot replaced it for her, though, out of his own pocket. He felt responsible, somehow."

"You reported all this to the police?"

"Oh yes," said Margaret Wilmot. "At least my husband did. But they could hardly spend all day defending our little shop, could they? I believe he also went to the Canadian High Commission to report the threats to them, though I'm not sure. We're still Canadian, of course." She was struggling now; her voice was so weak it was almost a whisper.

"We will go now," said Liz, "but may I ask you just one more question? Did your husband ever mention the name Dr. Julian Cox?"

"Cox," whispered Mrs. Wilmot, "Cox. No, no, I don't believe I've ever heard the name."

Sergeant Roy Carpenter let himself into his small third-story flat. He really had to get that lock fixed soon; the bolt was so rusty now it wasn't sliding across properly. He slung his red and white gym bag on the floor, went into the kitchen, and pulled a Labatt Blue out of the fridge. Carpenter thoughtfully screwed off the top and wandered into the living room. He leaned back into the couch, throwing his long legs over the coffee table. It had been a great day for a run. But it was awfully hot in here today. The apartment building's centralized heating was turned up far too high for such a sunny day. Still, he much preferred the English climate to that of his hometown of Grande Prairie, Alberta. He had gotten out of there as quickly as possible after high school. Why on earth his parents had left Toronto for Grande Prairie he never knew, and they had never given him a satisfactory answer. He had always wanted to visit England, and this posting had been a welcome one. He loved the sense of history of the place and the vastly differing accents, and enjoyed being called 'luv' by women he didn't even know. He had managed to visit a number of different parts of Britain on weekends off and was planning a visit to Manchester in the near future. While the posting didn't have the excitement of Bosnia, it certainly had its compensations.

The liaison officer took a long drink. Boy, that Lahaie was touchy, he thought. Roy had wanted to ask him about that hospital business in Bosnia for a long time. After all, Roy had himself been in Bosnia, hadn't he? Assigned to the International Police Task Force. Now *that* had been a job. Of course Lahaie had already left Bosnia by the time Roy began his posting there. But Roy had always been curious about those rumors of sexual misconduct at the hospital. And nobody would tell him anything. Colonel Lahaie had been in Bosnia at the time of the allegations; the supposed perpetrators were even in Lahaie's battalion, for crying out loud. So why shouldn't Roy ask about it? What was the big mystery? Running into Lahaie like that at the gardens, all casual, it had seemed like a good time to put the question. Wrong. Either something else was bugging the good colonel or Roy had hit a nerve somewhere. He took another long pull on his beer and closed his eyes.

Political Section Head Harry Jarvis was at his desk, not quite knowing why. No one was expected in the office today, and of course no real work could be done without subordinates. Jarvis was staring at a draft report from one of his officers. Everything he had told the police was true, of course. He rummaged in his desk drawer for a red pencil. Except that he had neglected to tell them what had happened a year or two *before* Guévin had deep-sixed his promotion.

What had occurred then—some years ago—was that Natalie Guévin, the bitch, had rebuffed him, rejected him, *spurned his advances*, as the romance novels say. He had agreed at first that it was for the best; she had put him off gently enough and it was true that her divorce was only recent. But then a tremendous, all-consuming, passionate hatred had begun to burn. Who was she to reject him? To say no to him, of all people? He'd even been senior to her at the time, although the cow had turned that around quickly enough. Must have slept with half the department to get promoted over his head.

So of course he had bad-mouthed the bitch. Done his best to blacken her name in the department. Innuendos, slurs, double entendres had all been quite effective. He had enjoyed himself for a time but eventually tired of the game. Then there had been that business with his promotion, when she had put the knife in. How could she stoop so low?

Of course, it had been his duty to report Guévin's affair with Carruthers to the security people at Foreign Affairs. He was pretty sure he had been the only one to twig to it, but then he had always kept a pretty close eye on her. It was conceivable that Paul Rochon knew about the affair, but he was very discreet. Guys like Paul had to be, didn't they? Oh well, she was gone now. Got what she deserved, no doubt, the whore. Jarvis went back to reading the draft, gnawing on the end of his red pencil.

Hay and Forsyth walked slowly back down the path to his battered Rover 2000. They were lost in thought, oppressed by the sadness of the tiny woman in the little bungalow. As they got into the car, their silence was broken by Wilkins's voice crackling over the radio. "Sir, we've been trying to reach you. We've been round to Cox's, sir. He's disappeared."

SIX

Anthony Thistlethwaite was sitting at his kitchen table, making a list of things to do before the Christmas reception. *Brief waiters. Set up Christmas tree. Ensure furniture in living room is moved.* He was trying to concentrate on his work plan, but his eyes kept straying to the newspaper lying on the corner of the table, the one with the headline blaring, ECO-MADMAN MURDERS MERCHANT!

Anthony, a thin, highly strung man, couldn't believe that the man who murdered Natalie Guévin had committed another such crime, and against another Canadian national. He wondered if there was a serial killer on the loose in London, and, indeed, how many murders one had to commit before becoming an official serial killer. The article made a convincing case, explaining how Canadian hunting and trapping techniques had been mimicked in the commission of both murders. It was ghastly.

These eco-warrior types were clearly a bit off, Anthony reflected—even dangerous, perhaps—but you never thought about them being a gang of serial killers. He wondered when it would end. At least security had been tightened at the High Commission and Residence, which was a relief to Anthony, but he wondered how well members of the general Canadian community in London were sleeping these days.

He was feeling very sorry for High Commissioner Carruthers, whom he held in considerable esteem. Carruthers had been very fair and kind to Anthony since being appointed High Commissioner to London. Some of Carruthers's predecessors had been downright cruel and had left Anthony wondering how they could have been accorded such a prestigious appointment. As chauffeur, he knew that a head of post's true colors came out if the official vehicle was held up in traffic on the way to an important event, and as butler, knew that any glitch in official entertaining could bring out the worst in the most benign of diplomats. Carruthers, however, was consistently calm and considerate, although the same could not be said of his wife. What Carruthers apparently lacked in spite was more than made up for by his beautiful, bitchy wife. Although, thought Anthony, as he flicked his pen between his long, nervous fingers, he had met her type before. Always best just to nod and agree and promise to get it right next time.

He looked at his list again, adding items automatically, but his mind was still full of murder. *Check bar supplies. Purchase new supplies as necessary. Find large tub for Moose Milk.* He almost added "try to placate Luciano" to his list; the talented chef was showing definite signs of strain these days. Then he said aloud, "Oh yes—polish the silverware." That should have been Annie Mallett's job, but she hated it and always did a substandard job. So it was left to him. He added that chore to his list as well.

Even during the morning meeting, Forsyth found something a bit odd about Hay. He seemed moodier than usual, quick to pounce on the smallest oversight of even the least-experienced constable. She glanced over at him, then watched, fascinated, as he mutilated a paper napkin.

The first order of business would be to locate Dr. Julian Cox. So far they had no leads: his ex-wife professed no knowledge of his whereabouts, his associates were playing dumb, and his apartment had yielded no clues. "The cat," commented Wilkins, "wasn't talking." The media had already made the apparent environmentalist link between the murders and was show-jumping to its own conclusions. As to the note found in the Hyde Park locker, it was thus far a blind alley. It could have been generated by any computer found in the High Commission—or almost anywhere else for that matter—and produced by as many printers. So it was back to interviews to try to determine Guévin's mystery man. Liz reflected on how simple the days of typewriters must have been—when an A with a missing lower half could solve a crime. At least that's what the mystery novels said.

Liz wasn't sure why she always felt compelled to jolly Hay out of his sulks. When the investigation team had been dispatched and they were seated alone at the table, she asked airily, "Zee leetle gray cells, zey do not co-operate zis morning, Detecteev Chief Inspector?"

He slowly raised cold eyes to meet hers. "I could have you up on charges for hindering an investigation," he said quietly.

"What on earth are you talking about?" she asked, shocked. She had no idea what was bothering him, but his tone was almost threatening.

"Go ahead and have your little joke, Forsyth. I have a few contacts of my own, you know, and I've used them. So don't play silly buggers with me."

The room was spinning slightly. "Calm down, Hay. I don't understand any of this. Talk sense, will you?"

"I'm talking about Middleton. About what he's really doing here. Ring any bells, Inspector?" he asked sarcastically.

"And just what might he be doing here?" she asked, flinching imperceptibly. She was on guard now, wondering what was coming next and wishing she had never heard the name Middleton.

"You want me to bloody spell it out, do you?" snarled Hay. They were both on their feet now. "I placed a call to a contact in Special Branch over the weekend. He rang me back this morning. Seems there was some talk of a love affair between Guévin and the good High Commissioner."

"Carruthers," said Liz dully. This made some sense.

"It was seen as some kind of security risk, you see, by your Foreign Affairs people. Presumably that rates as a foreign affair." But he wasn't smiling at his joke. "That's what Middleton is doing here, isn't it? Trying to find out if Carruthers had anything to do with the murder? And you with your cutesy little fake love letter. You knew about it all along, didn't you?" He was staring at her, hard. "Didn't you?" he repeated loudly. They remained there, motionless, for a fraction of a second.

Liz was astonished by her own reaction to this accusation from her British counterpart. She was part angry, part offended, and even a little bit frightened. "And what do you think gives you the right to go snooping around behind my back?" she asked, frozen. "It never occurred to you to come to me with your suspicions instead of going straight to Special Branch?"

Stephen Hay suddenly felt exhausted and dropped into a chair.

"If your source was half as good as you think he is," Liz continued, voice shaking slightly, "then you would know that I had no knowledge of this whatsoever. If this is true, there will be hell to pay back in Ottawa. But let me observe that it appears *your* people didn't keep you in the loop, either. Meanwhile, Detective Chief Inspector, I trust this browbeating is at an end. I'll get Middleton."

Hay remained still for a time. He believed she was telling the truth and wondered why he had been so angry. He had not intended to get so worked up, but then, he had always felt strongly about betrayal. He stood up slowly. He needed a cigarette.

Gerry Middleton was annoyed. He had been enjoying a nice breakfast at the hotel, only to find himself summoned like a child to the High Commission by that RCMP inspector woman. Must be having a bad hair day. The tour bus for Hampton Court was leaving in an hour, and Gerry had no intention of missing it. He'd never been to Hampton Court. *Whatever this is, they better make it quick*, he thought as he entered the Brandy and Cigars room.

Gerry missed that bus, and the next one, and the next. When Gerry left the High Commission he was no longer interested in visiting Hampton Court. He was too worried about what his boss would say when informed that Gerry's quiet little mission had been blown wide open.

"I trust," said Inspector Liz Forsyth coldly, "that you believe me now when I tell you that until today neither I nor my organization had any knowledge of either the liaison between the High Commissioner and Natalie Guévin or Gerry Middleton's real objectives here."

Hay nodded. It had been clear from the interview that Middleton had been working for Foreign Affairs, and Foreign Affairs alone, in privately confronting the High Commissioner about the affair. "Look, Forsyth, I—" he began but was not allowed to finish.

"We'll call Carruthers in now, shall we?" she asked, stone-faced. Hay nodded again. Gawd, he'd really messed this one up.

The High Commissioner arrived and shut the door behind him. His clear light blue eyes swept the room nervously, finally settling on DCI Hay. "I understand that you have been made aware of my affair with Natalie Guévin," he opened immediately. "I admit it."

As if you've any choice, thought Hay, then said, "Take a seat, High Commissioner."

"We loved each other, very deeply," continued Carruthers, sitting down. "I wouldn't want you to think this was a casual affair." He leaned forward, forearms resting on the table. "Things went . . . sour . . . between Sharon and myself some time ago. Natalie was a beautiful, gentle person, and I came to love her very much." His eyes were beginning to glisten. "I planned to leave Sharon once this posting was over. There was only about another six months to a year left anyway."

If you last that long, Hay said to himself.

"This note was written by you, then?" Liz asked, producing the crumpled paper. Her *cutesy little fake love letter*—wasn't that what the Scotland Yard bully had called it this morning?

"Of course. Natalie was getting fed up. She was tired of sneaking around, tired of all the stress. She had started to believe I didn't really care about her because I didn't want to tell Sharon. But if you knew Sharon—well, you'd know it's not quite so simple."

Hay and Forsyth unintentionally exchanged a glance.

"Anyway, Natalie broke it off with me as a result. I guess she thought I was weak, or insincere, or both."

"When was this?" asked Hay.

"A couple of weeks before Sharon and I were scheduled to go to Edinburgh. I was miserable. I don't think I'd really realized how much I loved Natalie until then. So I screwed up my courage and I told Sharon. Then I wrote the note to Natalie. She agreed to meet me later that night—at a little pub in the East End—and we made up."

"And how did Mrs. Carruthers react to the news?" asked Liz, genuinely curious.

The High Commissioner reflected a moment. "Strangely enough, Sharon had already guessed. She thought it was funny."

"Funny?" asked Liz.

Bang goes Forsyth's theory on the nature of women and adultery, thought Hay, although he had to acknowledge that the reactions of a Sharon Carruthers might well be atypical.

"Because it gave her a certain degree of power over me, you see," Carruthers continued. Liz regarded him quizzically. "You know how these things work. The person who's *in* the wrong becomes somehow enslaved by the person who's been *wronged*. Partly out of guilt, partly out of shame, partly out of fear that his misdeeds will be made public. When Sharon found out, it put her in the driver's seat."

"And then you went to Scotland with your wife after all this?"

"Oddly enough, Sharon insisted," said the High Commissioner. "Her stipulation on the entire affair was that, publicly at least, everything should remain the same. We would continue to live together, to go on holiday, to attend functions. We would still be a couple. Nothing would change until we returned to Canada. Then she would divorce me. At considerable cost, of course. I agreed to those conditions. I didn't have much choice."

"Tell me about Gerry Middleton," said Liz suddenly. "Is it true that you worked together in the past?"

"Heavens no. The first time I saw him was the day you arrived. That Parliament Hill business was just for your benefit. He came here to talk to me, to see if there was any possibility I might be involved in this thing. He knew about the affair—his people in Ottawa knew—but it only became an issue because of the—because of Natalie."

"And what did you tell Mr. Middleton?"

"I told him that I had been deeply in love with Natalie. That we planned to marry. And that I could never, ever have hurt her."

"And are you telling us the same thing now?" asked Hay.

"I am."

"And you were to say nothing to us about the affair?" asked Liz Forsyth.

"That's right," he answered. "Foreign Affairs thought it would be best kept quiet, so long as I had nothing to do with the murder."

And they, thought Liz, *believed that only they were in a position to decide that.*

"Do you know a Dr. Julian Cox, High Commissioner?" asked Hay suddenly.

"Of course. I've known him for some years. His specialty is cultivating government officials and then doing what he can to humiliate them publicly. Quite a charming fellow, really, and genuinely committed, but he'll do anything, step on anyone, for publicity."

"When did you last see him?"

"Last month, at the Canada Trade Fair. Cox and his band of merry men were there to protest against our fur industry. It got a bit rowdy, actually, and Natalie got shoved about a bit before the police intervened. All of our security personnel were of course busy hustling our minister out of harm's way, and Natalie was stranded for a few minutes."

"She must have been upset."

"At first, of course. But her reaction to Cox has always been much the same as mine. He's a major pain in the butt, and you can never, ever trust him, especially if the cameras are rolling. But you have to respect the guy. Anyway, as I recall she was a bit preoccupied around that time and didn't want to make a fuss about it."

"Preoccupied? How so?"

"She was going through a period of wanting to get a better handle on her personal roots. She'd immigrated to Canada as a baby, you know. She had just managed to re-establish contact with some relations in the former Yugoslavia—around Pale, I think she said. Seemed they were pretty well connected too. One of them—a cousin, I believe—came through London about that time as I recall. They got together for an afternoon. Anyway, all this was on her mind quite a bit. So, yes, she was somewhat preoccupied, distracted."

"And this incident at the Canada Trade Fair, that was the last time you saw Cox?"

"Saw him, yes," replied Carruthers. "But he left a message on my voice mail the day of the—murder. God, but that word is hard to say now. Used to be just another word. Now it has some kind of hold over me. Sorry. Anyway, I wasn't really sure what the message was all about. I'd intended to ask Natalie about it later. He said something about being sorry, the Internet page hadn't been his idea, some of his guys were going a bit over the top lately.

Apologized. As I say, it didn't make a lot of sense to me at the time. I think I saved it, though, if you want to hear it."

Hay nodded. "Mr. Carruthers," he said, "your wife would have us believe that Natalie was—rather promiscuous."

Carruthers gave a little laugh. "Nothing could be further from the truth. That was Sharon's idea of having fun at Natalie's expense, and mine. And then she convinced herself that if you believed Natalie was involved with lots of men, you wouldn't focus on just one, let alone the High Commissioner."

"She was trying to protect you?" asked Liz.

"She was trying to protect herself. She didn't especially want to be a focus of a public scandal involving her husband and his murdered mistress."

"But you didn't try to clear it up," said Hay. "You didn't try to set *us* straight. Why was that?"

"You're right," acknowledged Carruthers. "I thought perhaps Sharon's reasoning might be sound. Middleton thought so too."

"One last thing," said Hay. "Did you know that Natalie Guévin was pregnant?"

The news hit Carruthers like a blow to the chest. He blanched and remained silent for a long time. He looked like a condemned man. "Pregnant?" he finally whispered. "Was she?" Hay nodded. "I had no idea." The High Commissioner paused again. "So it was a—a double murder. A double homicide."

"You believe that you were the father?" asked Liz.

"Oh yes. No question." He thought for a minute. "How far along was she?"

"About twelve weeks."

Carruthers nodded to himself. "I wonder if she even knew."

"We've asked you this before, High Commissioner, but can you think of anyone who might have wanted to kill Natalie Guévin?"

The High Commissioner shook his head. Then he added bluntly, "Normally, I should have said my wife. But she was in Scotland with me at the time, wasn't she?" Carruthers, now quite pale, confirmed that he would remain available for further questioning and departed.

"What a very weak man," muttered Hay when the High Commissioner had left.

"Weak? For waiting so long to tell his wife about the affair?" asked Liz.

"For allowing the reputation of the woman he supposedly loved to be destroyed, just to save his own political skin."

Annie Mallett was in the dining room, dusting and snooping, snooping and dusting. It was the first time she had been allowed back inside since *it* happened. The door to that big anteroom, the one where all the coppers met, was shut again. The High Commissioner had closed it behind him when he left, looking sad and thoughtful. He hadn't even said hello to her, even when she greeted him with a polite, "Good morning, Your Honor."

She was dusting the big sideboard now—the mahogany one close to the anteroom door. Shifting some ornaments and a large Inuit carving to one side, she began slowly polishing the rich wooden surface. She edged a bit closer to the door, trying to hear what was going on inside the room and dusting all the while. Annie didn't know how it happened. Truly she didn't. When that carving hit the floor, she told Ethel and Sybil the following Saturday, you'd have thought a bomb had gone off.

Hay flung the door open with a startled "What the bloody . . . !" but stopped himself when he saw Annie recoiling from the carving (itself unharmed in the incident) in horror. Mercifully, just then the phone rang inside the anteroom and the detective chief inspector slammed the door shut.

Hay was still shaking his head as he picked up the phone.

Liz listened to his side of the conversation. "Yes, Wilkins. You've what? Good show! He's *where*? Serious? I don't bloody believe this. Yes, yes, go on then. See you later." Hay turned around slowly to face Liz, his mouth twitching a little. "You'll not believe this. They've found Cox. He's in prison in Hampstead. For setting off a stink bomb during the drinks and pâté at the annual Winter Hunt Banquet."

SEVEN

They were being painfully polite with each other now.

"Of course, Detective Chief Inspector."

"If that's how you wish to proceed, Inspector Forsyth."

"As you wish, Detective Chief Inspector."

Something had been lost during the confrontation. A degree of ease, a fragment of confidence, perhaps.

Wilkins and Ouellette, finishing their debriefing on Cox's activities in Hampstead, shared a look. The mood in the anteroom, Wilkins thought, was better suited to a French farce than a police investigation.

"Couple of kids," muttered Ouellette, as he and his partner headed out for a late lunch. As they left the High Commission they were almost bowled over by an angry-looking heavyset man charging into the building.

"Who the heck is that?" asked Ouellette, regaining his balance and staring at the back of the big man.

"No idea. Maybe the murderer, come to turn himself in," suggested Wilkins. "He'd better improve his manners, though, if he wants to get anywhere with the genteel Hay and Forsyth today. Anyway, probably just a Canadian who's lost his passport."

With a quick backward glance to ensure the man had been stopped by the security guards, Ouellette nodded. "You're probably right. Let's get lunch."

Hay and Forsyth were reviewing background checks on Dr. Julian Cox and some of his closest associates in preparation for their interviews later in the day. Their strained silence was broken by a deep, heavily accented voice.

"My name is Miroslav Lukjovic," he said. "And I want to take body of my daughter back to Canada."

"What's so special about bleedin' tourtière anyway?" fumed Luciano Alfredo Carillo. "Looks like meat pie you can buy in any corner shop." The High Commission chef glared at the recipe book. As if he didn't have enough on his mind making canapés for over two hundred for the Christmas reception. Now he had to build a stockpile of Canadian meat pies as well. Probably eaten with maple syrup on the side, he sneered to himself. No wonder his predecessor had left. Whatever happened to old Gunther anyway?

Of course, he brooded, he could use some help, assistance—an experienced saucier perhaps. But no-o-o-o. All Carillo heard when he broached the subject was an earful of blather about cutbacks, downsizing, reduced budgets. What did all that have to do with *haute cuisine*, that's what *he* wanted to know. He slammed the pastry onto a well-floured board. This Christmas party was in very poor taste anyway, he thought. So soon after a murder right here on the premises. He began rolling out his dough with a mighty display of passion.

"These invitations look fine, just fine, Mary," said Paul Rochon, handing back a randomly picked selection of twenty or so. "I'm sorry I don't have time to look at all of them, but they look very good. Absolutely correct. And you have such lovely handwriting."

Paul looked more tired and anxious than usual, thought Mary Kellick. She believed the Deputy High Commissioner to be working much too hard. Mary flushed and bobbed her head, saying, "Thank you, Mr. Rochon. Shall I send them out with the drivers, then?"

"Yes, please, Mary. Good job." Paul watched her disappear out of his office. She had lost all confidence since that balls-up a few months back, and it hadn't helped that Sharon Carruthers now insisted that Paul double-check all of Mary's work. It was a shame she had to be humiliated like that.

It wasn't fair to him either; he was swamped as it was. He'd already lost a couple of so-called "person-years" this year. Why couldn't the government just call them what they were, anyway? They were staff positions, people doing important work and usually doing it very well. There were more cutbacks to come. This was all starting to hurt very badly. And what about Sharon Carruthers? Why couldn't she check the damned invitations herself? What did she do with all her time anyway?

He opened a thick file folder entitled "Visit of the Secretary of State for Foreign Affairs, Dec 18–20, '97." The High Commission, as he knew better than anyone, was already falling behind in its work due to the murder inquiry. There were two high-level visits scheduled in December, each with its usual briefing requirements, program of calls, hospitality, press, and logistical arrangements. Then there were the other visitors: the businessmen, the cultural figures, the occasional elite athlete. With reductions in staff it was hardly surprising that the real work of the High Commission wasn't being done. Who had time to advance foreign policy, to deal effectively with bilateral issues, to maintain multilateral efforts, or to thoughtfully analyze the issues when working as a glorified travel agent?

That headquarters was in the middle of yet another departmental reorganization made matters even worse: most of the high-priced help at Foreign Affairs were using their brains studying new reporting arrangements and organization charts, not working on foreign policy.

As always, the fact that Jarvis wasn't pulling his weight didn't help. Jarvis, thought Paul, seemed to spend all his time either red-penning the work of his officers or gossiping around the office. Well, the self-important political section head wasn't going to get much of a rating report this year. That was clear. Paul always tried to be fair, but so far Jarvis's aptitude for management merited a big C minus. How many times had Jarvis's officers come to see Paul, complaining of everything from benign neglect to abuse of power? No, this guy was a rotten apple, no question.

Paul was himself an old-school diplomat, a great admirer of the golden age of Canadian diplomacy, and was, in his own quiet way, doing his best to recreate it. Not that anyone seemed to care anymore. The professional work ethic with which he had been imbued as a young officer was giving way to the demands of unions and the personal grievances of individual officers. Nobody wanted to work overtime anymore simply to get the job done. Everyone wanted compensation for each little bit of extra effort. A functioning meritocracy was being turned into a swamp of mediocrity. Affirmative action for every conceivable minority group seemed on the horizon. Every minority group save his, that is. He still had to keep certain things in his own life very quiet indeed.

He sighed and started digging through his thick working file. He found the relevant piece of paper and began typing into his computer: *The High Commission of Canada presents its compliments to the Government of Great Britain and has the honor to inform . . .*

Miroslav Lukjovic sat at the table across from Hay and Forsyth. He was calmer now, less aggressive. The security guard who had accompanied Lukjovic withdrew after a curt nod from Hay. Here was simply an old man who had just lost his only child. Liz had promised to look into getting the body released as soon as possible, and her apparent empathy had gone a long way toward soothing the big man.

"I know I am making nuisance," he said, "but it seems unfair. I am far away. In Montreal. I just want her back. I believe High Commission is responsible for—what word— *repatriating* body to Canada. This is why I come here."

"Of course," said Hay smoothly, "and we are doing our best to get to the bottom of this terrible crime." Lukjovic nodded, staring into the cup of coffee that sat before him. "Do you think," Hay continued, "that you are up to answering a few questions for us? The more we understand your daughter, the greater our chances of finding the killer."

"Certainly." The heavy man nodded again. He was probably in his early seventies but was unexpectedly vigorous, carrying himself with the masculine grace of an over-the-hill boxer. His skin was taut across high cheekbones. His English was ponderous and broken in places, but he was somehow articulate.

"What you want to know?" he demanded, then immediately answered his own question. "Natalia is our only child. Olga, my wife, almost die with her, so no more. Back in old country, this. We love her. She is smart, pretty, always in the mischief." He smiled at some half-forgotten recollection. "When we—leave—what was Yugoslavia, we come to Montreal. She learn French. She sound French. Of course she forget old country. They do, the young. They forget." Lukjovic's eyes were sorrowful. He was continuously clenching and unclenching his thick fingers.

"She went to university in Montreal, I think?" asked Liz.

"Montreal, and Quebec City too. Like I say, very smart girl. I want her to be lawyer. But she decide to be bureaucrat. What to do?" he added with a shrug of his shoulders.

"And you were close to her during those years?"

"Sure. Sure. We have many disagreements, of course. You know young."

"What type of disagreements, Mr. Lukjovic?" asked Hay.

"Type of disagreements young and old have always. Love. Politics. Is normal."

"Love, Mr. Lukjovic?"

"Yes." He waved his hand. "She want marry young man. I say, 'He is not right one, Natalia.' But she marry anyway. Then she divorce couple of years later, yes? Thanks God no children."

"You are speaking of her ex-husband, Philippe Guévin?" asked Hay.

"Yes, of course," replied Lukjovic. "Young think only they know love. Not true. Only old understand, really. I know. You know one day, Chief Inspector."

Hay wondered for an instant whether that were true, then asked, "And politics? What did the two of you disagree about politically?"

"Ah," said Lukjovic, "politics. She don't care about old country, see? She say, 'Papa, we are Canadian now. This not our battle.' She don't understand, see?" A tear rolled down the old man's face. He continued, "My family still there. Friends. Is terrible war, much suffering. I know what happens there. People tell me. I want to help. But Natalia, no, she is Canadian. She don't care. We have—words over this. Many times. Upset my Olga. But, it is young again, see? They see world different way. It is same, all time. What to do." The old man's head dropped. He suddenly seemed very tired, very old.

"You don't need to continue, Mr. Lukjovic. I understand this must be very difficult," said Liz.

"I thank you." He nodded. "Is long airplane from Montreal. I must rest. But before, I have other friend of Natalia to see. They ride horses together in park. I go find this Colonel Lahaie. Do you know where is his office?"

Dr. Julian Cox, co-founder of the Eco-Action group, publisher of *Ecology Now* magazine, and mastermind behind the already infamous Hunt Banquet stink bomb incident, had been transferred to Scotland Yard about an hour ago. He lounged comfortably, smoking his pipe and waiting to be questioned about the murders of Natalie Guévin and Lester Wilmot. Hay and Forsyth were running late, but Cox wasn't in a hurry. This was all quite entertaining, really. Moreover, recent events had proved a downright blessing for the cause. The press had connected the environmentalists with the murders almost before the police had, and now the papers were full of items on ecology, the issues and the movement. *No such thing as bad publicity*, he mused as he waited patiently in the small interrogation room. Very clever murders, too, he smirked. The second one, with the *collet* motif, had been particularly inspired.

The interview lasted an hour and a half and left Hay and Forsyth seriously frustrated. "Cool as a cucumber, that one," commented Liz, as they walked out into the damp. "No alibi, no defense. He didn't even seem to care if he got charged with a double murder."

The rain had been steady earlier in the day but had tapered to a light drizzle as evening approached. Now it was gloomy and oppressive, and not a ray of sunlight was capable of penetrating through the heavy cloud. Hay opened an umbrella as they made their way to his car.

"My great-aunt's canary could have come up with a better alibi," Hay agreed. "Went out 'for a walk' for a few hours after Ouellette and Wilkins left? Just around the time of the Wilmot murder?" Hay shook his head. "Doesn't look good."

"Surely he could have come up with something better than that. Or is he being too clever by half? Anyway, I'm not paid to be a lawyer. Can you charge him?"

"I wish I could. I can't stand that guy, with his hairy little grin and his holier-than-thou attitude," grumbled Hay.

"If a holier-than-thou attitude were a felony offense, half the Canadian Parliament would be in jail," Forsyth said.

He looked down at her, but it was too dark to see if she might be smiling. It had been a painful day, with all its unpleasantness and forced politeness. His part in it made it all the worse.

"Anyway," he said, "all we have for the moment is circumstantial. I want around-the-clock surveillance." Hay was driving his aging Rover back into town. "Look, Forsyth," he began, "let me say my piece here and now. I was well out of order this morning. I was utterly in the wrong, and I want to apologize. I'd send flowers, but you'd probably feed them to your horse." Liz couldn't help smiling at the image. Hay continued, "I do ask you to consider how you'd have felt in my size twelves. I felt I'd been double-crossed. But I was out of line and I apologize."

"That's alright. Received and understood. Let's forget about it." But no, she didn't think she'd take him up on his offer of a drink. A cozy pub on a rotten night like this was exactly what she needed, but she was still stung by what she had taken to be the very personal nature of Hay's attack.

Mary Kellick felt better than she had for several days, better than she had since the murder. She was making chicken cacciatore tonight, so she was finely chopping a large green pepper, just like the recipe said. Hadn't Paul Rochon been kind to her? He had only checked a few of her invitations, so she would know he trusted her. He was nice, Paul. He had seemed intimidating at first, but that was because he was Deputy High Commissioner and the rank was quite awe-inspiring. Paul was nice, a bit like Natalie. He talked to Mary, said hello. It made her feel like she fit.

Mary smiled to herself. She wasn't feeling quite so tired, quite so muddled up these days. It was a good thing she had stopped taking those tablets Dr. Barnes had prescribed last summer. They only made her groggy and a bit nauseous. She hadn't taken anything for about three weeks now, and look at her: she wasn't depressed at all. Feeling quite cheerful, really. She measured a teaspoon of oregano, a quarter teaspoon of pepper, and a quarter teaspoon of thyme into a little dish, then stirred the spices carefully into a bowl of tomato sauce. Mary Kellick felt just fine.

Liz sat alone at a small table in the dimly lit dining room of the Roxborough Hotel, toying with a glass of

Merlot. Only one other table was occupied, by an elderly couple seemingly on a first date. What an idiot she was, she thought, lighting a cigarette. Her wounded pride and some undefined hurt had led her to turn down the offer of a friendly drink, and now here she was, alone on her *birthday* for Christ's sake.

She couldn't believe that she had completely forgotten her own birthday. The case, the Middleton affair, the interviews with Cox and Natalie's father. And the incident with Hay. They had been getting along so well, too. She could cheerfully strangle Middleton for landing her in this mess, but he had prudently checked out of the hotel earlier and disappeared, doubtless back to Ottawa, without a word. *Hasta la vista, baby*, she thought, vowing to have his hide when she herself returned. So here she sat, turning forty-four, alone in London. "Talk about cutting off your nose to spite your face," she muttered to herself.

Her waiter—was that French accent real or not?—presented her with a basket of assorted breads, setting it on the starched linen with a flourish. She had never understood why some women complained they were ill-treated when dining alone in restaurants. Liz had never found that to be a problem. Maybe it was because she routinely over-tipped. That was another myth: women were lousy tippers. So Liz had launched a one-woman crusade against the stereotype.

She had been crusading around for a while now, she reflected. Not that many women study criminology. *I'll do that.* Not many women in the Mounties. *I'll do that.* Not many women make inspector. *I'll do that.* (The last, of course, was not all that simple, but Liz was making a point here.) She wondered if Natalie Guévin might have been a bit the same. There weren't a lot of senior women in the foreign service either. And look where it had gotten Natalie.

The waiter—who was, in fact, French—went back into the kitchen. What a quiet night this was. He'd be home by ten at this rate. At least the customers were nice this evening, not like some he'd had lately. That old couple, out for their celebration. Quite touching, really, to know the old folks can still have a good time. And what was that pretty little woman doing in here all by herself? Maybe here on business. Perhaps some kind of executive secretary or something. She didn't look very happy, though, smoking her cigarettes and staring at the tablecloth. He hoped she was one of those women who left a decent tip, anyway.

She must stop being so gloomy, she thought. This was her birthday, after all. A celebration of sorts. Time was an odd concept, she mused, realizing immediately how trite that thought was. Sometimes it crawled: she had sat through meetings that seemed longer than the average lifespan. Yet here she was, in her mind only having joined the RCMP weeks ago, but now closer to retirement than recruitment.

She looked over at the elderly couple, who were laughing and clinking their glasses. The woman with the pretty white hair and soft laugh was gently flirting with her partner. *So, what am I to be celebrating now?* The good news, of course, was that she was back in London. She had loved it here when she had come back for the first time, as a teen. Maybe there was some kind of law enforcement exchange program or something, and she could work here for a while. That way she could ride in Hyde Park whenever she wanted.

She had enjoyed her ride with Colonel Lahaie; perhaps she could fit in another while she was here. And that Anglo-Arab mare had been an excellent ride, though challenging. Something in her temperament reminded Liz of Centurion, the black gelding with which she'd been partnered during her musical ride days. Lahaie was an interesting man, and very charming. Hay could take a few lessons from the colonel. What an interesting life he'd had.

She found herself wondering what had really happened with that hospital business in Bosnia. It had rung a bell when the colonel had mentioned it. The papers had been full of Bosnia for some time; she must have read something somewhere. She let out a ragged sigh. She wasn't sure what was bothering her, apart from the fact that there were two bodies in the police morgue and one or two murderers on the loose. Something else was bothering her.

Hay was bothering her, for one, she thought. She'd come across his type before: moody and grumpy, thought that the quality of his mind would make up for his personal shortcomings. If she were honest, she'd almost been frightened of him this morning. Some old instinct, born of some past pain, had raised itself up to protect her from a man who, for an instant, had seemed menacing.

She was being unfair. She knew that Hay hadn't come close to threatening her, that doubtless he'd be horrified to know the thought had crossed her mind. She knew she was overreacting. Hay was just something of a grouch, that was all. With a finely tuned sense of humor, too. He seemed to find her funny anyway. Not everybody did. She suspected that some people thought her a smartass.

The smoked salmon arrived, and the smiling waiter topped up her glass. So what if she was spending eighty percent of her per diem on smoked salmon, she thought. It was her birthday, after all.

"Bon appétit, madame." Accent sounded real enough. Accents. That Miroslav Lukjovic had one heck of an accent alright. Sounded like something straight out of a John le Carré novel. He mustn't spend a lot of time with non-Yugoslav Canadians. Although perhaps his French was more fluent than his English. Hadn't he said that Natalie had gone to school in French?

Liz wished her French were better. She had learned that being considered "officially bilingual" didn't carry a lot of weight when visiting Trois-Rivières. She had been taught French as a child in Calgary and had continued with it during her university years. Nonetheless, her attempts at speaking French to francophones did not seem to be welcomed very graciously. She must ask Ouellette if her accent was really all that bad.

She chewed her smoked salmon thoughtfully, watching the couple at the other table. They were now deep in conversation. What were they talking about so earnestly? She and Rick had started out having wonderful conversations but had run out of things to say after about six months. Her thoughts returned to Hay, as they sometimes unexpectedly did these last few days. Maybe he wasn't so bad after all, just terribly passionate about his work. Maybe he was really quite a passionate man. She supposed these intense, inward types might be like that. *Good grief*, she thought suddenly. *This must be their anniversary. Certainly the waiter is offering his congratulations.* Thirty-five years? *Thirty-five years and she's still flirting with her husband?*

Damn, what was bothering her? What had she been thinking of a few minutes ago? The case, yes. Lahaie. The hospitals. Lukjovic. *The papers had been full of Bosnia.* That was it. The papers had been full of Bosnia. And so was this case, Liz suddenly realized, pushing away her half-eaten salmon. This case *was* full of Bosnia.

EIGHT

They were being kicked out of the High Commission. It was inevitable, of course, but Hay would miss the Brandy and Cigars room all the same. He stuffed some documents and his own sheaf of notes into his battered briefcase, recalling how poor Thistlethwaite, wearing his butler's hat, had apologetically explained that Madame wanted the reception areas cleared in anticipation of the Christmas reception. Hay was relieved that it had been Thistlethwaite, and not She Who Must Be Obeyed herself, who had relayed the message.

Hay had acquiesced immediately, of course. There was no way his superiors would want to turn something like this into an international incident. There wasn't much more they could do on these premises now anyway.

It was only 7:40 AM, according to the wall clock. Hay was first on the scene as usual. He had not spent a restful night, despite a quiet evening reading Molière and sipping a nice Glenlivet. Both had almost but not quite prevented him from reliving that nasty scene with Forsyth. What had fueled his unexpected anger yesterday morning? He had even surprised himself. It was out of character, and it bothered him. He must keep himself under greater control.

Worse, he had felt yesterday that for a brief instant he had actually frightened her. It might not have been fear, of course, but after so many years on the force he was familiar enough with that look in the eyes. He thought he had seen that look yesterday, very briefly, and had been both shocked and baffled by it.

Finishing his packing, he dropped into the overstuffed armchair patterned with yellow and white sunflowers. It was peaceful here this time of morning. The slow ticking of the antique clock and familiar gurgle of the coffee urn were all that he heard. There was no Annie Mallett, at least not yet, dropping *objets d'art* and making sheep's eyes. Thistlethwaite was clearly already on duty, and doubtless that odd little chef was banging about in the kitchen. But here, at least, it was silent.

He looked at the little stack of envelopes on the table. As some sort of compensation for their eviction, he supposed, he, along with Forsyth, Wilkins, and Ouellette, had been invited to the Christmas reception. Thistlethwaite had said that representatives of the diplomatic community were expected, as were some British officials and other figures, cultural and academic, who were particular friends of the High Commission.

Hay didn't much care for formal functions, but it might be interesting to see if all diplomats were as glum as this lot. It wasn't just the shock of the Guévin murder, either. He had never seen a workplace so full of strain, of fatigue. Paul Rochon, the deputy, looked like he was on the brink of collapse. And Mary Kellick. There was something very odd about her. She seemed so nervous that she might shatter into pieces at any moment. And that Jarvis was a little weasel. He had been virtually leering at Forsyth throughout his interview. Just last Friday, he realized. It seemed a million years ago.

"Good morning, Hay," said Forsyth, appearing in the doorway.

"Good morning, sir," said Ouellette, heading straight for the coffee urn.

"Good morning," said Hay. He stared at the young sergeant, who was pouring spoonfuls of sugar into a cup. "What happened to you, Ouellette? You look like hell."

Liz grinned. "Self-inflicted injury, I suspect."

Ouellette leveled a bloodshot gaze at his superiors with some difficulty. The bluish circles underneath his red-rimmed eyes were in stark contrast with the unusual pallor of his skin. He felt a throbbing in his temples and a creasing pain around the middle of his forehead. He was surprised by a slight tremor in his fingers as he picked up the china cup, and quickly rattled it down again.

"Rather a late night last night, sir. Ma'am. Wilkins thought that since it was my first time in London, I ought to see the sights."

"And which of our famous sights did he choose to show you?" wondered Hay aloud. "The Victoria and Albert Museum, perhaps? Our Wilkins is quite the culture vulture, you know. Or would it have been Whitehall? Maybe the Tower of London?"

Liz smothered a laugh.

"Not exactly, sir," replied Ouellette weakly as he sat down carefully at the table.

"Well, at least you've got the intestinal fortitude to turn up. I wonder where my own good detective sergeant might be right now?"

"I'm here, sir," said Wilkins from the doorway. Wilkins was wondering why no one else seemed to find the ticking of the wall clock preternaturally loud this morning.

Colonel Claude Lahaie was typically the first to arrive at the High Commission, military tradition dying hard as it does. He leafed through his morning traffic, which appeared to consist largely of irrelevant reports from other capitals. The staff were all back at work now, of course; the workload didn't evaporate simply because there had been a murder on the premises. The High Commission, however, remained in a state of collective shock. No one was really back up to working speed. How could they be, with murder so fresh and the police still encamped on the premises? Not to mention that the murderer was still on the loose.

Lahaie fired up his computer, reflecting back to the weekend. It had really been most pleasant. Sunday, especially, had been a beautiful day for a walk. He looked forward to his wife's return from her vacation in Victoria, where she was visiting her parents. She was a rock, and there were some disturbing things going on. The murder, certainly. Then that unpleasant incident with the sniveling Carpenter in the park. Lahaie hadn't liked Carpenter much to begin with, and he certainly had no time for him now. Sniffing around about that hospital business. Who did he think he was, a bloody journalist? And who said a war zone was supposed to be a Boy Scout camp anyway? *Peacekeeping is a bit tricky when there's no peace to keep*, he reflected for the hundredth time.

It wasn't as though there hadn't been other things going on in Bosnia, both before and after his own tour. Like the rumors of that drug operation a year or two ago—who had bothered to follow up on that? They always wanted to know about the bleeding hospital. It wasn't the Somalia Affair all over again, that was for sure. There had been nothing to it. Nothing to it at all. Anyway, that was all in the past now. Dead and buried. Lahaie inhaled deeply, then turned back to his stack of telexes.

Sergeant Gilles Ouellette was waiting in the elegant lobby of the Roxborough Hotel for a car to take him to Heathrow. His head still hurt, and he was damnably thirsty. He certainly hadn't been prepared for Inspector Forsyth to ask him to return to Ottawa for a few days. He wasn't in shape for it either, not today—no matter how interesting the assignment.

He would bounce back, though, he knew. Ouellette was not a tall man, but he was tough and stocky, with the build of a hockey player. Which he had, in fact, been, almost through to the National League. Eventually deciding he would rather use his head for something other than being rammed into the sideboards, he had joined the Mounties. He had done well, had made sergeant at a relatively young age, and had served in three detachments across the country prior to going to Ottawa. He would have been very surprised to learn that he had left a string of broken hearts and angry recriminations across the country; it wasn't his fault if his personnel people kept posting him before he had a chance to get serious.

At the moment, he was thinking that Forsyth got some

awfully funny ideas. Now she was convinced there might be a few too many Bosnia connections in this case. She'd asked him to go back to do some digging. Check in the files at the RCMP, Foreign Affairs, National Defence, the Canadian Security Intelligence Service. "Speak to whoever will speak to you. Find out about that hospital business, any other rumored improprieties, the alleged drug-trafficking operation. Check into Lukjovic, and get the security files on his daughter. Have a good look at Lahaie, as well as at Carpenter and anyone else at the post who has ever been stationed in Bosnia."

It was hardly surprising that Bosnia had come up once or twice during the course of the investigation, he thought. After all, Canada was often involved in peacekeeping operations, and it seemed that many members of the Canadian forces had served in Bosnia at one time or another. The RCMP as well—Ouellette knew personally a number of guys who had been over for a tour. And Canada, as was often remarked, was a country of immigrants. Natalie Guévin's background came as no surprise. There might be something to it, but he wasn't sure it warranted his returning to Canada. At least not when he felt like this. Surely Forsyth could have done this by telephone.

He had seen that Hay found the idea interesting, although he hadn't said much at the time. Ouellette liked the British DCI. He thought his boss did as well, but he didn't have a clue what was behind yesterday's behavior.

They'd been going around all day like a cobra and a mongoose, although it had been unclear which was which.

God, he was in no shape for this. Not today of all days, with his head ready to crack open at any time. Wilkins's fault entirely, of course, he smiled ruefully, with his beer-tasting tour of historic London. But it had been a good night out. He liked Wilkins a lot. Maybe Wilkins would visit Canada later this year, and Ouellette could provide a reciprocal headache. Although he wasn't sure if Wilkins could get away from his girlfriend—what was her name? Oh yes, Gemma. Odd name, thought Ouellette, but then this was England.

He flipped through his airline tickets. The High Commission had been very helpful in arranging them so quickly, he thought. He checked his watch, making the calculation. It was the middle of the night in Ottawa. With any luck, he could sleep a bit on the plane. And he would stick to orange juice this time.

They had managed the move over to Scotland Yard quite painlessly. No one from the High Commission had said anything. Unless one counted Annie Mallett, who had managed to pull Hay to one side, stating emphatically, "You don't look at all like him, you know, which is a shame, but then you're the type that grows on a girl, aren't you?" Hay had not known what to say, or even what the housemaid was talking about, so he had smiled faintly down at her, nodded his head, and fled.

Liaison officer Sergeant Roy Carpenter was treating himself to a couple of days off. He'd been filling in for his own boss, on medical leave in Canada, for over two months. He'd contributed more than his fair share to the increased security at the High Commission and had been pulled in several times to take notes for the police. He was exhausted. A few days in the north of England would do him a world of good. He would make it back in time for Friday's reception, of course. The High Commissioner's Christmas party was a command performance.

He had forgotten his Nikes at the High Commission and asked his driver to wait as he picked them up. Walking back down the front steps, out of the office and off on vacation, he felt like a free man. Suddenly a heavy hand smashed onto his right shoulder. Whirling around, Carpenter found himself looking straight into the watery eyes of Miroslav Lukjovic.

"You, security man," Lukjovic growled, "you Royal Canadian Mounted Police. You here to protect my daughter. To keep eyes on her. You not do your job this time, Sergeant."

Carpenter shook himself free of the old man's grasp. "I'm very sorry about your daughter. There's nothing anyone could have done."

Carpenter ran quickly down the walk and sprang into the waiting vehicle. Lukjovic stared balefully at the car until it disappeared from view.

The exacting, detailed, at times mind-numbing work of the murder investigation was now well underway. Background reports were compiled and scrutinized; alibis were checked and double-checked. Speculation as to motive was intense: some believed that an environmental activist as fervent as Cox might easily be driven to homicide; others thought that the brutality of Guévin's murder, at least, screamed a personal motive. Opinion was equally split over the question of whether they were dealing with one murderer or two. Hay held the mandatory press conferences and hated every minute.

The crimes were re-enacted endlessly, the forensic evidence reviewed, the psychology of possible suspects dissected. The angle of the blows was examined in detail. As was the probable type of knife. The possible suppliers of the wire used to garrote Wilmot and of the ax handle used to club Guévin were painstakingly researched. That the club used on Guévin had been left behind but the knife never found strongly implied a political motive. The killer had not wanted the police to miss the symbolism. Hay and Forsyth certainly hadn't missed it, and Dr. Julian Cox remained top of the list of suspects. He was under twenty-four-hour surveillance but had lately done nothing unusual, at least not for an activist. Everything pointed to Cox, but there was no hard evidence. His alibi for the first murder seemed to hold up. His associates were prepared to vouch for his whereabouts at the time.

He could not be placed at the scene at the time of death: he had vacated the premises by 5:17 PM, according to the Embassy log. One of the security personnel, McFaddon, had signed him out.

A detailed investigation of the physical security—locks, cameras, hardware—of the High Commission and Residence had been conducted, and it was difficult to imagine that anyone could have either broken in or re-entered the premises without having been spotted. While it seemed that the first murder might well have been an inside job, Cox's alibi for the second murder was altogether suspect. Had his penchant for publicity led him to capitalize on the first crime by committing a second? The MO practically screamed eco-terrorism and anti-Canadianism. Lester Wilmot's killer appeared to have waited inside the fur store and taken Wilmot unawares. He probably entered the store when there were other customers about, secreted himself behind some of the racks of furs until Wilmot closed up, then slaughtered him. There was a drawer full of prints from the store now as well, but none matched any of those found in the anteroom. The killer had doubtless worn gloves.

The Eco-Action website and its affiliates had been analyzed, and a clear trend toward greater radicalization of the movement over recent months had emerged. Cox had been true to his word on one count: Guévin no longer appeared as an "enemy of the environment." Cox had been severely beaten by sealers in Quebec in the past, which may have resulted in a serious grudge against Canadians. The message left on the High Commissioner's voice mail was played and replayed. But there was no definite physical link to either of the crimes—nothing solidly linked Cox to either crime, and nothing clearly linked the two crimes together.

Cox's apartment had been thoroughly searched at the time of his brief disappearance, but nothing much had been found. The death threat letters to Natalie Guévin had never turned up. How had the press so quickly—within a few hours—linked the murders? Were they just awfully clever (Hay dismissed this thought as soon as it occurred to him), or had they been tipped off by the killer? That would indicate one murderer, and they were back to square one.

There were others with potential motive in the frame, for the Guévin murder at least. These included the High Commissioner himself, possibly wanting to ensure that word of their affair never went any further. Sharon Carruthers was another possibility. She might well have wanted her rival dead.

A team had been dispatched to Edinburgh for a minute-by-minute follow-up on the activities of Wesley and Sharon Carruthers while in Scotland, but the police team was taking longer than anticipated to trace the couple's movements. This was partly because Hay and Forsyth had agreed that this particular aspect of the investigation should be undertaken discreetly; Hay in particular was concerned that it might be tantamount to the *rattling of skeletons*. But there were also some curious gaps. That no one at the hotel could recall seeing Mrs. Carruthers between early Wednesday afternoon and early Friday morning was of particular interest to Liz.

Harry Jarvis was another possibility. Jarvis seemed to have detested the victim for career reasons and, it seemed, for others. Jarvis's loathing of Guévin had been corroborated by a member of his own staff, who went so far as to suggest that Jarvis had been behind a whispering campaign aimed at Guévin some years back. "A quiet kill," he had called it, although he noted that, in the long run, Natalie had not been irreparably harmed. Hay and Forsyth were open to the possibility that Jarvis might have done it, but his alibi stood up. At least, his Russian host maintained that Jarvis had been at his reception all evening. It would, however, be checked out yet again.

The interviews that other members of the investigative team had conducted with the rest of the High Commission staff had yielded little of interest, but many would need to be interviewed again, probably by Hay and Forsyth this time. According to the first series of interviews, in addition to the security staff, there had been twenty Canadian staff members as well as fourteen locally-engaged staff on the premises at the time of the murder. All claimed to have been working late, and all would have had unimpeded access to the Residence dining area during that time. Staff working late at the High Commission would not necessarily leave by the front door; there was more than one exit from the office, and the others were locked from the outside but not guarded.

All security personnel present on the night had been interviewed at length, and they all claimed that nothing had appeared out of the ordinary. They confirmed a tacit understanding that Mary Kellick was permitted to perform her "rounds" every night. The Carrutherses rarely if ever used the dining room and kitchen areas in the evening unless they were hosting an official dinner. The household staff, the only ones who had been close to the scene at the time, were never under serious consideration.

One of the weaker alibis was that of Colonel Lahaie, although he was vaguely remembered by a waiter at the tandoori restaurant. "He might have been here" were the waiter's exact words. But Lahaie had no discernible motive. He had been right in one respect, though: several of the High Commission staff hinted at a supposed love affair between Lahaie and Guévin. Paul Rochon's suggestion of *an intruder, a nutcase*, was looking better all the time, Hay thought, although it would have taken an awfully clever intruder—a magician, even—to get past the High Commission's security systems.

They began to think again about Mary Kellick. The girl was intelligent, highly sensitive, and extremely nervous. But could this possibly have led her to commit so grotesque an act? What would have been her motive? Would she even have been strong enough? They brought in a police psychologist. Kellick was interviewed and pronounced probably incapable of such violence. "Probably?" muttered Liz. "And this guy cost how much?"

If the picture at Scotland Yard was murky, a snapshot of the High Commission would have depicted virtual chaos. The staff were frightened. What they had initially assumed to be some kind of personal vendetta against Natalie had rapidly taken on political, anti-Canadian proportions. Canadian and British staff were fearful now, less inclined to work late despite the heavy load, more preoccupied with their own safety.

The Canadian community in London and throughout the rest of the country was similarly alarmed. Some residing in London, especially those with any connection to the fur trade, decided to return to Canada for a while. Others moved up the dates of their vacations and left the country. The High Commission was inundated with calls from Canadians resident in London and elsewhere, asking for advice and updates, asking what the High Commission was doing about this, and demanding new passports in record time. Staff members were told not to count on Christmas leave.

The forthcoming visit of the foreign minister was on, then off, then on again. There was much wringing of hands in Ottawa as to whether the minister might be in danger in London, or whether it would be deemed cowardly for him to stay at home. Paul Rochon duly scheduled meetings and events, canceled them, then scheduled them once more. The visit of the Canadian finance minister later in the month was similarly in flux. The Canadian Film Exhibition in early January was definitely off, but the team of auditors who were to descend on the mission on January 15 was, unfortunately, still on the cards. There was no question about the High Commission Christmas reception, however. It would take place as scheduled on December 16; Sharon Carruthers said so.

Worst of all, the Privy Council Office and the Prime Minister's Office were following events closely, demanding constant briefings and updates, to the consternation of Foreign Affairs. The British Foreign and Commonwealth Office was similarly discombobulated. They had hoped, much as had DCI Hay, for this to be an internal High Commission matter with nothing to affect the state of bilateral affairs. The eco connection had them deeply worried. There had been complaints from several Embassies during the past year about Eco-Action, but the Foreign Office had initiated no action against the organization, largely for fear of domestic repercussions. Publicly, they hoped for a quick resolution. Privately, they prayed that the murderer carried a Canadian passport.

The task force itself was working like a well-oiled machine. Liz was impressed by the professionalism and dedication of the officers of the CID, and she came to realize that part of their enthusiasm was born of their abundant respect for the detective chief inspector. It was considered a bonus to work with him. Hay and Forsyth had managed to surmount the earlier unpleasantness and were working well together now, with an ease and humor that infected the more junior officers assigned to the case. But this didn't alter the fact that they were getting nowhere.

When Sergeant Ouellette began his researches in Ottawa, he was quite surprised to find himself greeted as something of a minor celebrity. Events in London had been receiving such wide coverage, and had become such a preoccupation in government circles, that Ouellette was given unbridled access to files held by all the relevant agencies as well as to all personnel. Desk officers to senior managers were more than willing to talk to him; everyone seemed to hope that they held the one piece of information that would crack the case.

Ouellette had run into Middleton briefly at Foreign Affairs one afternoon after lunch at a nearby pub. Not up to English standards, he thought, but it didn't do a bad job. Middleton hadn't looked particularly pleased to see the sergeant, had muttered a brief greeting and fled. Ouellette didn't know why Middleton should feel so uncomfortable: no mention had been made in the papers of Guévin's involvement with the High Commissioner. CID could be discreet as well. Ouellette spent most of his time reading through files, making notes, and trying to piece together as much information as he could. He was starting to think that perhaps his boss might be on to something after all.

DS Richard Wilkins was having difficulty finding the Bull's Head pub in the dark. It was raining, as usual, and the DCI's directions seemed somehow incomplete. He was supposed to meet the boss and Forsyth for a drink, although why Hay had picked this out-of-the-way place was beyond the youthful detective sergeant. He shifted back into second gear, peering at the numbers on the nearby row houses.

Even in his wildest fantasies, Wilkins could never imagine being anything but a police officer. From the time he first learned to play cops and robbers, he insisted on being the cop, and he had never found any reason to learn a new game. Wilkins was a good officer, maintaining a remarkable psychological balance for someone in law enforcement. Wilkins didn't understand the seemingly complex psychology of his boss, not by a long chalk, but he was delighted to be working with the moody but insightful detective chief inspector.

Wilkins was single, but not for long if Gemma, his girlfriend, had anything to say about it. His beloved had been dropping hints for so long that it was only a matter of time now. She may have had a point—even Wilkins was prepared to accept that. They had been more or less engaged for two years, but something always came up to prevent him from making any serious plans. The words *how convenient* were often enough on Gemma's lips, especially when Wilkins's work snatched him away at a particularly sensitive moment.

She hadn't been very happy about being left alone tonight, either, he reflected. But he had very much wanted to join the others for a review of the case. If he could just find the bloody pub.

The Bull's Head was an old-style establishment, more to be expected in the countryside than situated in the heart of London. Oak-beamed and dimly lit, with wooden benches and a long, comfortable bar, it had quickly been adopted by Hay some ten years ago. The locals, being largely working folk, had originally greeted the arrival of a CID copper with some suspicion. That was some time ago. Hay was now part of the landscape.

The landlord, Billy Treacher, had bought the Bull's Head out of love. He had been a regular for years and had jumped at the chance to purchase the pub when the previous owner decided to sell. Billy had steadfastly refused the encroachment of anything resembling music, television—especially the large-screen variety—or, worst of all, video games. Video games were somewhere along the road to damnation. The ale was good, the food was mediocre, and the pub was everything it should be; moreover, that was how the punters liked it. The Bull's Head would retain its integrity as long as Billy Treacher survived.

Hay's arrival at the pub with a slim brunette caused several heads to turn, but by and large the regulars were a discreet lot. Settling into a booth late Thursday evening, they continued their discussion of the case.

"It's quite sad, you know," said Liz, "but my impression is that Natalie Guévin never really did anything especially wrong in her life. Falling in love with a married man, maybe, but that's not unheard of. Yet we can sit here blithely imagining all sorts of reasons for people to want to kill her."

"It's not the first time I've thought that, either," said Hay, before tasting his pint. "When you spend a lot of your life conducting murder inquiries you find there are a lot of motives out there. Luckily, not everyone acts on them."

"How long have you been in, Hay? You're starting to sound like Moses."

"Twenty-eight years," he said. "I joined up when I was twenty-four, having just finished a second degree. And before you ask, French literature. And before you ask again, no, I don't know why."

"Regrets?"

"Is this where I do the Frank Sinatra shtick?" he asked. "'I've had a few.'"

"No, I'd like to hear you do Piaf. I can just see you belting out 'Non, je ne regrette rien.'"

Hay smiled and lit a cigarette. "You?"

"Oh yes," she said. "More than a few regrets in my case."

Hay wanted very much to ask her what she meant. It was difficult to accurately read her expression through the gloom. Hay usually came here by himself and had never really realized how dark it was. But before he could speak, Wilkins found them.

"There you are." He said with a broad smile. "I had a helluva time finding this place, but at least I could tell it was you two from the clouds of smoke over the table. You right for another drink?" They nodded and he disappeared again.

His moment missed, Hay said, "He looks like a lost puppy since he lost his mate. Those two were becoming good chums. Anyway, your lad should be back soon."

Liz nodded. "We spoke briefly today. He's going to call me tomorrow on a secure line when we're at the Residence for the reception. *Damn!*" she said suddenly.

"What is it?" he asked, startled.

"Oh, nothing," she mumbled, but Hay thought her face might be flushing a bit in the dark. "It's just that I have to go out and buy a—dress, that's all. For the reception. I didn't bring a dress uniform; why would I? So I'll have to go as a girl."

That shouldn't be too hard, thought Hay, but he said nothing. You couldn't say anything to women these days.

Wilkins returned with the drinks. "You heard from Ouellette lately?"

"Oh, right. That's just what I was going to tell you. He's

calling me tomorrow with a full report. Said he found some interesting stuff, but he needs to do some more work and then he'll call us at the Residence during the reception. Oh, and he finally got his bags. They'd been routed through Lisbon for some reason best known to the airlines."

"I do hope he's come up with something interesting," said Hay. "I had a few lights going off about that Bosnia angle as well, but I wasn't so quick to put them all together."

"Comes of spending your birthday on your own, I guess." Then she almost bit her tongue off.

"What's that?" said Hay, taken aback. "When was your birthday?"

"Why didn't you let anyone know?" said Wilkins, concerned. "We could have at least gone out somewhere."

Liz muttered something about having wanted a quiet night at the hotel, but she saw Hay putting two and two together. And now he felt bad. *Damn*, she thought, *I didn't want to dredge all that up again.* She said lightly, "My own fault. Don't like acknowledging the years. Er—nice pub, this, isn't it? What's it called again?"

Hay was watching her closely. He answered slowly, "It's called the Bull's Head."

"Well," said Wilkins cheerily. "We'll come back for a real celebration another time." He raised his glass. "But here's to you. Many happy returns, Inspector Forsyth."

NINE

Luciano Alfredo Carillo had a massive headache and it was only eight o'clock in the morning. Two hundred and fifty guests. *Two hundred and fifty*. Hungry, and arriving at seven o'clock tonight. This was impossible. What did they think he was? A miracle worker? Of course, there were dozens of fully loaded trays in the freezer; he and his small crew had been working like things possessed all week. But some things could only be done on the day. Like the melon and prosciutto kebabs. And the caviar-stuffed quail eggs. The stuffed mushroom caps. The deviled chicken livers.

Where to start? Carillo sat down at his little wooden table, head between his hands, and moaned. Where to start? Thank God at least he had all those Canadian meat pies.

Liz hated shopping. She hated it back home, and she hated it here. She stood in the tiny cubicle, her clothes in an undignified heap on the floor. Liz looked at herself in the mirror. Every book that Liz had read when she was young contained the line, "She smiled at her reflection." Liz wasn't smiling. The pink monstrosity that she was wearing looked exactly like what it was: a party frock. The frills and flounces were hideous, the color was silly, and the neckline was too low. She tore it off—the tenth today—and trudged to the next shop.

So far everything had been too young or too old, too tight or not tight enough, too colorful or too dreary. She was even past looking at price tags. She couldn't understand why some women loved shopping. To her, every dress that didn't work was a personal insult, a shortcoming, an affront. Liz didn't know why she cared, really. Who did she want to impress anyway? Surely not Hay, she thought. She wondered what Sharon Carruthers—whom Liz had privately dubbed "Morticia"—would be wearing, the cow. Probably something quite stunning and outrageously expensive.

Hay had surprised her again, earlier in the week, she remembered. She had decided she needed a ride to clear her head after a particularly graphic forensics briefing.

Having observed that horses were "great, unpredictable beasts with a nasty sense of humor," Hay had nonetheless offered to drop her off at the stableyard. When she returned from an exhilarating canter around the park with Reckless, she had been surprised to find Hay's Rover still parked there. He had been deep in informed discussion with old Albert Taylor about, of all things, thoroughbred bloodlines.

She entered what appeared to be a quality dress shop. When she re-emerged she carried a large bag containing something black and probably too short that had cost a week's salary. Now came the hard part. If there was one thing she hated more than buying dresses, it was buying shoes.

Annie Mallett rarely allowed herself to be stressed, but today even Annie was feeling the strain. Everything had to look *just so* when the guests arrived, and she had a lot of wiping and dusting and vacuuming to do. She had to do the big drawing room where the guests would have their cocktails and chat, as well as all the little rooms off to the side. The dining room and anterooms all had to be done because people always did spill over, didn't they. It would be difficult to dust, too, with those Christmas decorations all over the place. It didn't help that Mrs. High Commissioner kept following her around, criticizing and issuing instructions. Madame was in a bad mood today even for *her*, thought Annie.

And there sat Anthony Thistlethwaite, she thought, serenely polishing the silver Christmas candlesticks without a care in the world. All that he had to do tonight was see the bars were running smoothly and the waiters—hired especially for the occasion—were paid at the end of the night. Annie gingerly picked up the large Inuit carving that had fallen off the mantelpiece early in the investigation. She reddened slightly as she remembered the look on the detective chief inspector's face when he strode out to see what the racket was.

She picked up a clean rag and wiped the surface of the sideboard. Well, she wiped around the ornaments anyway. Annie wondered what Anthony would think if he knew she once believed him to be the murderer. He was, after all, the butler, wasn't he? She had told that nice detective chief inspector, too, but he had only thanked her for her assistance and told her he was very busy right now. Well, perhaps she had never really believed it was Anthony, but it had been a good excuse to go and have another look at the DCI. It was a shame he'd left, along with all his mates; life at the High Commission had been dead boring in the few days they'd been gone.

"I had no idea that would take so long," muttered Liz, entering Hay's office, where she had been installed since operations shifted to Scotland Yard. While she had initially felt uncomfortable about invading his privacy, Hay had been most hospitable, even succeeding in finding her a desk and chair in the storeroom.

"I'm glad you're back, Forsyth. I've just had a phone call from Mrs. Wilmot. She wants you and me to go over there as soon as we can."

Liz tossed her bags on the desk and trailed him back out the door. They were soon in the Rover heading toward Wimbledon. The rain hadn't let up since last Sunday, and the windshield wipers were slapping back and forth furiously. Hay was perturbed that he had left his umbrella back at the office. The car ashtray was full of butts, his and hers, and a good deal of ash had spilled onto the floor as well. "We should empty this ashtray," she observed.

"Or buy a new car," he said.

"No, you shouldn't," she objected. "It suits you. You're a bit alike, really."

Now what the hell, wondered Hay, *does she mean by that? Good quality, reliable, with a touch of class? Or over-the-hill, ill-maintained, and a bit cranky?* He wasn't sure what the answer would be, so he didn't ask.

It was difficult to drive in rain like this—sheets of blinding rain slicing across the windshield in great waves. "One of these days," he said, almost jumping an unseen stop sign, "I really must move to a better climate."

"Don't think about Canada, then. It's brutal. This is like paradise to me, for this time of year anyway."

Hay mumbled something, then almost swerved off the

road to avoid an oncoming car. "Where's that damned turn-off? I can't see a bloody thing. Oh, here it is."

They stood once again on the front stoop of the charming bungalow, this time like two drowned cats. Mrs. Wilmot answered the door, and now there was no Mrs. Jenkins to hinder them. Even the best of neighbors have their own lives to lead.

Mrs. Wilmot seated them graciously and brought tea. It was tranquil in the little sitting room, with its comfortable blue tapestry armchairs and book-lined shelves. No radio or television was playing. The only sound heard in the small room was that of the rain hurtling itself against the windows.

"Thank you for coming out, especially on a day like this," said Mrs. Wilmot softly. The hoarseness in her voice was gone. It had probably been due to too much crying, thought Liz. "I was sorting through some of Mr. Wilmot's things earlier today—papers and such. I've decided to sell up and go home, you see, so I needed to locate some documents. And I found something I thought you should see."

She reached into a legal-sized brown envelope and withdrew three sheets of paper. "These were hidden away at the back of his file drawer," she said. "I never went into Mr. Wilmot's files before, you see, and I've never seen these letters. He didn't show them to me. I expect he didn't want to worry me. He was . . . like that." She handed the sheets to Hay, who read them with considerable interest. They were of the type described by Colonel Lahaie—threats made up of words and letters cut from magazines. The first one read:

STOP TORTURING AND KILLING ANIMALS FOR FASHION AND PROFIT. NEVER UNDERESTIMATE US. CLOSE YOUR DOORS OR YOU WILL REGRET IT. WE INSIST ON ACTION NOW.

Liz looked over the other notes, which were largely the same. She agreed with Lahaie: they were a bit corny, but they were chilling as well, especially in light of Lester Wilmot's fate.

Hay looked over at Mrs. Wilmot, who was sitting silently, deep in her chair. He said unexpectedly, "Mrs. Wilmot, I am going to say something that perhaps I have no right to say. But may I ask you to reconsider, just for a while, your decision to sell up and go home?" Both Mrs. Wilmot and Liz looked at him in surprise. He continued gently, "It's always a great temptation after such a terrible loss to make a big change in your life. Please believe me when I tell you that such decisions are very often the wrong ones. You may well decide to return to Canada, but this may not be the right time to make that choice. I apologize for being so personal, but I would hate to see you make a mistake. And I wonder if Mr. Wilmot might not agree with me."

Mrs. Wilmot gazed at Hay for a long moment, then

gave him a grateful smile. "I don't know if you're right or not, Chief Inspector. But I will think it over, I promise you that. Thank you for caring to mention it."

Liz sipped her tea, experiencing an almost physical pang of guilt. She had fancied herself a little frightened of this man just a few days ago. Her instincts were all wrong these days.

"Well," said Hay, ducking the rain on the way back to the car, "we may have something to go on here." He slammed the driver's side door shut. "We'll have the lab boys go over these. I doubt there are any prints, but perhaps they can trace the typefaces to some particular magazine or magazines. Cox's publication *Ecology Now* would be a good start."

"At least it seems to tie the two crimes definitively together, even though we don't have the Guévin letters."

Hay nodded and almost knocked down a sodden cyclist. He hated this climate.

Mary Kellick was having trouble concentrating on her work. She was too excited about the reception tonight. Of course she would be on duty, like everybody else at the High Commission—ensuring everyone was fed and had someone to talk to—but it was awfully exciting just the same. All those important people, gathered together in one place, dressed up to the nines. This was the best night of the year, thought Mary.

She had been to the Christmas reception every year

since she had started working here. The Residence, she knew, would be festooned with garlands and twinkling with lights. And candles, lots of candles. Carols would be playing. One year there had even been a quartet of strolling carolers, all dressed up in Elizabethan clothes. But she doubted that would happen this year. She doubted that Sharon Carruthers liked strolling carolers.

Mary had only a tiny office, but it was comfortable and she liked it. There was even a view, of sorts, consisting largely of buildings, but then she knew she was lucky to have a window at all. Not even the diplomatic staff had windows. Her office was tucked away at the end of a long corridor, hidden from view. She had brought in some prints of flowers in vases, a calendar with photos of young animals in it, and several pretty houseplants, too, which seemed to like the office as much as she did.

She was compiling the proposed guest lists sent in by the heads of section for "A Reception in Honor of the Visit of the Secretary of State for Foreign Affairs," which was supposedly taking place on the eighteenth and nineteenth of this month. She knew the visit might be canceled again, but the work had to be done just the same. Mary was really thinking about what she would wear to the Christmas reception tonight. It was the biggest event of the year, and she had selected her floor-length black skirt with the buttons all the way up the front and her sparkly black-and-gold top with the high, stiff collar. She would wear her real gold hoop earrings and her new black pumps. That should be perfect. This was to be, after all, the best night of the year.

"I swear that woman will drive me mad!" cried Sharon Carruthers in the general direction of her husband. The High Commissioner was seated at his desk in the study, trying to read his morning traffic.

"What woman?" he asked absently, leafing through the pile of papers before him.

"That Mallett woman, of course." She flopped into a wing chair next to the desk. "Will you listen to me, Wesley? I want her fired, that's what. First thing tomorrow. At the rate she's going she'll still be dusting while the guests are arriving. Wesley?" Wesley Carruthers nodded and continued reading. "Wesley." Sharon Carruthers stood up again and leaned over her husband's desk. With one swift motion she swiped viciously at the stack of papers. They fluttered about for a while, then landed gently on the floor. "*Now* will you listen to me, Wesley?"

Hay and Forsyth were back at Scotland Yard, examining the letters given to them by Mrs. Wilmot.

"You know, Forsyth, I don't think we should hand these over to the lab boys just yet."

"No? Why not?"

"I think we should use them to bring in our favorite eco-warrior one more time."

"That's a good idea," she said thoughtfully. "We haven't really grilled the guy yet. Maybe we can get something more out of him this time."

"Shake him down, do you mean, Inspector?" asked Hay in mock astonishment. "You do surprise me. I always took you for such a civilized woman."

"I have my moments. But I promise to behave with total respectability at the reception tonight," she said gravely.

"Even in the company of Sharon Carruthers?"

"Especially in the company of Sharon Carruthers. You won't recognize me."

"This I've got to see," muttered Hay as he dialed Wilkins's extension.

Dr. Julian Cox was not altogether surprised to be called back to Scotland Yard, but he was somewhat inconvenienced. His small daughter, Samantha, was visiting, and now the little girl had to be dropped back at her mother's house en route. Samantha's delight at riding in a police car was matched only by her mother's shock at seeing her arrive in one. What she'd ever seen in that Julian, she thought, she'd never know.

Liz had never seen anyone quite so comfortable in an interview room. Even she was affected by its starkness and apparent isolation. It was even worse than those back home, but Cox might as well have been sitting in his own living room. "So, officers"—he had insisted on calling them "officers" the last time, too, Liz remembered—"what can I do for you today?"

Their pre-arranged game plan had no effect. Liz tried to empathize with Cox, to understand and to reason with him, while Hay tried to needle him, mock him, provoke some anger. No reaction. He seemed impervious. After some forty minutes of this, Hay, in frustration, shoved the three letters under Cox's nose. "What do you know about these?"

Cox glanced at the papers and replied, "They're mine. They look like the ones I sent to that furrier."

"Christ!" growled Hay under his breath. "And have you sent others? To Natalie Guévin, for instance?"

"Sure. And to a number of those other bastards as well. My daughter likes to make them," he smiled indulgently. "She likes gluing things to bits of paper."

It wasn't the most satisfying interview either of them had ever had, but at least Cox would remain in custody for uttering threats. "I wish I'd bloody asked him up front," said Hay. "What a bleeding waste of time. Come to think of it, maybe I should have just asked him straight out if he murdered Guévin and Wilmot. He might have admitted it." Their eyes locked in sudden surprise. *Maybe that wasn't such a dumb idea after all.*

Colonel Lahaie had picked up his dress uniform from his favorite cleaners. Spot Less was close to the Embassy and was run by an enterprising couple from Malaysia. Ali and his wife, Fawziah, were an attractive young pair who took great pride in their work. Everything came back clean, on time, and at a reasonable price. Theirs was the only shop in reasonable proximity that did uniforms. Lahaie realized with a small jolt that they also cleaned furs.

He was heading home early to help his wife, just back from her trip, with the Moose Milk. Just a particularly potent form of eggnog, but it had become an established tradition for Canadian military attachés to supply it for their Embassies' Christmas parties. Enough to intoxicate a battalion, thought Lahaie with a grin.

And transporting it to the Residence was always a major logistical challenge. His wife had bought enough ingredients to ensure a nasty hangover for the entire diplomatic community. He smiled to himself, thinking of Ruth. He had missed her when she was in Canada. He was glad she was back. Especially now.

They were reviewing the most recent press articles the case had inspired. "No," said Hay, shaking his head. "It sounded like a good idea for a minute, but even if Cox confessed would *you* believe him? Would *I*? I really think he's just attached himself to these cases for the publicity."

Liz nodded, chewing on a stale cheese sandwich. She missed the food at the High Commission. "I suppose you're right. I doubt even he could explain how he might have gotten back into the High Commission once he'd signed out. Maybe we should ask him, though. Might give us a few ideas. God knows we could use some." She paused. "Why aren't you eating anything? A pot of coffee isn't much of a lunch."

"Not hungry, I guess. Anyway, I guess we'll be fed tonight at the reception."

"Don't remind me. I don't really want to go to this thing. Do you?"

"Not really. But I guess we're committed." He paused. "Perhaps after we've put in an appearance we might move on to the Bull's Head, if you like. You did say you liked it."

Liz stopped chewing briefly. "Yes, yes, I think I'd like that very much." *Did something just change here*, she wondered. *Or am I just imagining it?* They both quickly went back to their press clippings.

TEN

The dress seemed even shorter than Liz remembered. Sighing, she piled her hair on top of her head and loosely secured it with a gold-colored clip she had found at Boots. She lit another cigarette and administered some makeup, on the grounds that any dress that expensive deserved a face adorned with a few cosmetics. As always, she was ready much too early. She had once seen a bumper sticker that read, PUNCTUALITY IS A VIRTUE, IF YOU DON'T MIND WAITING, and it popped back into her head now. She helped herself to an exorbitantly expensive Ballantine's from the mini-bar and waited for Hay and Wilkins to pick her up. Again, as always before going out, she wished she could get into her sweatpants and have a quiet night in front of the television. There was a good old movie on tonight, too: a Bette Davis at 8:00 PM. At least she had a quiet drink at the Bull's Head with Hay to look forward to, she thought, if she could just make it through the reception.

She liked this room very much and found herself wondering how much longer she would be staying there. Whether the case was solved or not, she couldn't stay on indefinitely. At the moment, it didn't look good. Hay was right: Cox made a doubtful suspect at best. More suited to throwing stink bombs than committing murder.

The phone rang loudly. Wilkins from the lobby. She grabbed her RCMP jacket, the only one she had with her, and shut the door behind her.

The Residence was glorious, decorated for the Christmas season and scented with pine. The Vienna Boys' Choir caroled from the stereo, and the twinkling lights gracing an enormous tree seemed to dance in time. All the wooden surfaces were gleaming, the silver was glistening in reflected candlelight, and couches and chairs had been tastefully rearranged against the walls to create more space.

Three fully loaded bars had been set up, and gallons of Moose Milk would be dispensed from a large tub, which sat atop a low wooden table adorned with pine boughs and ivy. The food and beverage waiters were in place; Anthony Thistlethwaite had seen to that. The High Commission staff, on duty early as if by unwritten law, were already clustered about in small groups, drinks in hand, speaking in hushed tones. They waited for their work to begin.

Luciano Alfredo Carillo had had a dreadful day, but he had pulled it off. The Valium that Thistlethwaite had slipped him had helped a little. Trays of delicate cold canapés were waiting to be served: tiny Swiss meatballs with a variety of dipping sauces, miniature sausage rolls, cherry tomatoes with fresh mozzarella. Other delicacies waited for a last minute warming in the oven: spanakopita, miniature samosas, mini crab melts. And tortière. Lots and lots of tortière. Luciano sat at his little table in the kitchen, surrounded by trays full of beautifully prepared hors d'oeuvres. For one golden moment, Luciano Alfredo Carillo was a happy man.

Mary Kellick sat at her kitchen table, tears flooding her eyes and dissolving her carefully applied mascara. She was wearing, as planned, her long black skirt with the buttons up the front, her sparkly black-and-gold top with the high collar, her gold hoop earrings, and her new black pumps.

But now she would not go to the Christmas reception at all. She was instead sobbing and gasping uncontrollably, and the room was spinning at lightning speed.

A few moments before, Sharon Carruthers had stormed

into Mary's apartment. She had seemed a raging demon to Mary, who had twitched her head rapidly in confusion and fear at Mrs. Carruthers's attack. At first Mary didn't understand what Mrs. Carruthers was saying. There seemed to be a lot of noise, and Mrs. Carruthers's glossy peach lips were moving quickly up and down and sideways, but Mary couldn't understand a word. Then things slowly came into focus and Mary heard her saying, "What do you mean you forgot to send them out, you stupid little cow?"

"But we called everyone," Mary whimpered, "and everybody will come. I must have left some of the invitation cards here at home, and they weren't sent out. I worked on them here, you see. But most of them went, really. People are arriving anyway, aren't they? We phoned everyone." She was nodding quickly, up and down, hoping to convince this Fury.

"You dense little moron!" screamed Sharon Carruthers. "You stupid, witless imbecile! Get out of here!" she shrieked, momentarily forgetting that she was in Mary's apartment. "I don't want to see your stupid face ever again! Get out! You're fired, finished!"

With that, Sharon Carruthers had spun around and left as quickly as she had arrived.

"Wow!" exclaimed Wilkins, eyeing Liz approvingly. "You look fantastic. No wonder the Mounties always get their man!"

She laughed and looked up at Hay a bit hesitantly. "Yes, you really do look lovely," he said quietly. She did, too. There was something of a Botticelli painting about her tonight, although he wouldn't dream of saying so. He had, after all, completed all the mandatory courses in gender awareness. They hailed a taxi to the High Commission. It was well within walking distance, but one didn't get gussied up like that to trudge the streets of London.

The guests had begun to arrive. Wesley Carruthers, handsome in black tie, greeted them in the reception hall, accompanied by a radiant Sharon Carruthers, swathed in peach silk. Ambassadors, generals, and ministers filed through the entrance. The tempo of activity increased slowly, as did the noise level, and almost imperceptibly the reception began acquiring its rhythm. It all looked so effortless.

Once inside, the three of them stayed clustered together, clutching their drinks. They were not altogether comfortable in the company of the other guests, most of whom they had never seen before and some of whom were on their list of suspects. Liz made a valiant if doomed attempt to mingle at one point, returning to her companions quite quickly. "What happened?" asked Hay.

"It went something like this," she said. "I said hello. They said, 'Hello, and what brings you to London?' I said I was investigating a murder, and then they suddenly saw all kinds of people they knew on the other side of the room." She sighed. "I knew this wasn't likely to be my kind of crowd."

"So I take it you won't be doing that again?"

"I won't. Guess who I saw over there, though. Natalie's father, Lukjovic."

"What's he doing here?" Hay asked, partly to himself. "I thought he'd be back home in Montreal by now. We released the body a couple of days ago."

"I know. He muttered something about having some unfinished business here in London. He was in a hurry—seemed to be looking for somebody. I think he's already gone," she said, scanning the room.

Sharon Carruthers suddenly shimmered up. "Oh, I'm *so* very glad you could come," she crooned. "Are you enjoying yourselves?" Of course they were, they said, very much. "And, my dear, don't you look *lovely*," she continued, looking at Liz. "And aren't you *tiny*? I didn't know Mounties came that small," she said with a tinselly laugh.

Hay was certain he felt Liz become totally rigid by his side. But he wasn't about to look at her.

Sharon Carruthers continued, "I see we have a couple of *smokers* here. You should be careful of that, my dear. Bad for the *wrinkles* you know." She patted her own dewy cheek. And then she was gone.

Liz said nothing, even though she felt she was about to explode. Hay clamped his hand down on her right shoulder, holding her in place. "Now, Forsyth," he said, "I've already got two homicides on my plate. I don't need a third."

She whirled to face him, but he didn't relinquish his grasp. She said seriously, "Do you remember, Hay, that I once told you I wished Sharon Carruthers was the murderer?"

"Yes. Yes, I do," he said.

"Well, I wish to retract my previous statement. Now I wish she'd been the bloody victim."

Hay started to laugh. He'd found himself laughing more than usual lately, despite the circumstances. "Don't let her bother you. She's only envious, you know."

"Envious?"

"Of course. She can't stand being outshone at her own party."

Liz flashed him a grateful smile. Hay could be downright charming when he wanted to be. She excused herself and was rather more composed when she returned from the ladies' room, where she had indulged in unspeakable thoughts about Morticia Carruthers. Colonel Lahaie had now joined Hay and Wilkins and was looking manly and graceful in his dress uniform complete with gold braid.

"There she is," said the colonel, "and looking wonderful."

"The colonel here has just passed on some rather interesting information," said Hay.

Liz looked quizzically at Lahaie.

"Yes," he said. "I was just chatting with my French

counterpart over there." He nodded in the direction of a colonel in the French army. "We're members of the same squash club. So is your friend Dr. Julian Cox, by the way. Anyway, my colleague mentioned in passing that he played squash with Cox last Saturday. Of course, he didn't think much about it—why would he?—but then I'm following the investigation closely. When I pushed him a bit, he said it was late in the afternoon. Between four and six. If I'm not mistaken, that was about the time of the Wilmot murder, was it not?"

Liz nodded slowly.

"I thought you would want to know," said Lahaie.

"It looks like the little bugger had an alibi alright," said Hay, shaking his head quickly. "He just didn't want us to know."

"So that we would keep him in the frame," said Liz.

"And he'd get the publicity," added Wilkins.

This was discouraging. While Cox had not been the best of suspects, he was the best they had. They stood awhile, digesting the information and conversing, then Lahaie asked Liz if she had tried any of his Moose Milk. Liz shook her head, and Hay and Wilkins watched as the colonel piloted her toward the tub of potent alcohol.

"Noxious beverage, Wilkins," Hay remarked, watching Lahaie and Forsyth disappear into the crowd. "Ever try it?"

"No, sir."

"Don't bother. But you should try one of these," he

said, taking a slice of tortière from a passing tray. "The meat pies are good."

Sergeant Roy Carpenter was fuming. He had missed the earlier train from Manchester, and there was no car to meet him at the station. Now he was in a taxi and already very late for the reception. He still had to get changed. It had been such a great little holiday—what a way to spoil it. He leaned back in the taxi and tried to relax, but he found it difficult.

Mary Kellick was slumped over her kitchen table. Her pale right cheek, laced with sodden mascara, lay against the cheerful blue and white checks of her tablecloth. A gold hoop earring was digging into the side of her face, but she didn't notice. Mary Kellick would very soon be dead.

"Did you enjoy your Moose Milk, Forsyth?" asked Hay.

"It's pretty powerful, that's for sure," she said. "If I start dancing on tables just take me home." She gazed about the glittering room with its glittering guests, then asked no one in particular, "Where's Kellick, I wonder? Shouldn't she be here?"

A High Commission security guard tapped her lightly on the shoulder. "Inspector, it's a Sergeant Gilles Ouellette from Ottawa. He's on the secure line. You can take it in the High Commissioner's study if you like, ma'am."

"Oh, right. I can't believe I almost forgot. Must be the Moose Milk. You guys coming with me?" she asked, turning back to Hay and Wilkins.

They didn't need asking twice: some police work was genuinely welcome compared to the discomfort they felt with their current company. The security guard led the way. Once inside the study, he pointed to the apparatus on the High Commissioner's desk and handed Liz the key. She had a clear line to Ouellette almost immediately.

Hay and Wilkins sat on a couch in the study for what seemed an exceptional length of time. "Good thing we brought our drinks," muttered Wilkins.

Liz was listening very intently and scribbling a great many notes on a pad she had found on the desk. Finally she said, "You don't mess about, do you, Ouellette? I'm not sure what all this means, but it's great work. When do we expect you back? Tomorrow? Good. See you then. Thanks again."

Sergeant Roy Carpenter had just changed into his dress uniform. Damn—he would be very late for this reception. He hoped he could sneak in without Sharon Carruthers noticing.

The deafening crash puzzled him for a second, immobilized him. Then he heard heavy footfalls in the hallway and realized what was happening. He really should have fixed that lock. They were on top of him in a moment—the younger, stronger one with a sharp, cold blade to his throat.

The young man pulled Carpenter to his feet, pushed him down into a chair, and took up a position behind him. The knife pressed into Carpenter's flesh all the while. The older man pulled up a chair across from Carpenter. He fixed Carpenter with a watery gaze and said, "So. Now you tell me why you want kill my Natalia."

Liz turned to her companions. "Okay, here goes." She consulted her notes, realizing they were largely illegible. "First, Lahaie was right. There was nothing to that hospital business. A couple of minor events blown way out of proportion."

"Oh, good," said Hay.

"Second, as we know, there have been persistent rumors of an international drug-trafficking operation out of Bosnia. It goes something like this. The drugs originate in Central Asia and are routed through Russia to Bosnia—an easy run due to the instability and lawlessness—and on to the West."

"Go on," said Hay.

"Ouellette stumbled across some other rumors, not widely circulated. There may even have been involvement by some members of the International Police Task Force in the drug operation."

"But wasn't Sergeant—" began Wilkins.

"Exactly," said Liz. "The name of one Sergeant Roy Carpenter, currently of the High Commission in London, came up more than once in those files. Nothing ever stuck; there was never any proof. But the rumors persisted. And the fact remains that he was attached to the International Police Task Force in Bosnia during the time the rumors of trafficking were at their height."

"Good God," Wilkins gasped. "What the hell have we got ourselves into here?"

"There's more, isn't there, Forsyth?" asked Hay intently.

Liz drew a breath. "Yes. It seems that most of the drug money from these operations has ended up in the hands of a small group of Serbian nationalists residing in the West. They turn the cash right around to finance the war effort." She paused. "And the name that pops up most frequently in that connection is . . ."

"Don't tell me," groaned Hay. "Miroslav Lukjovic, of Montreal, Canada."

Liz nodded and flopped back in the leather desk chair, dazed.

Hay was thinking hard now. "Where's Carpenter?" he snapped suddenly.

"I don't know. I haven't seen him tonight. I had heard he was going away for a day or two."

"But he couldn't miss this, could he?" said Wilkins. "Shouldn't he be here?"

"I hope I'm wrong about this," said Hay, jumping to his feet. "But I think we had better find Carpenter fast, or that lad could be in a lot of trouble."

Hay, Forsyth, and Wilkins raced out of the Residence so quickly that they scarcely had time to wish their hosts a Happy Christmas. They hardly noticed that the noise level of the reception had increased markedly, as had the sound of laughter, as the Moose Milk did its useful work. Sharon Carruthers wished the trio a Merry Christmas, her Peach Passion lips twitching slightly as they left.

"Look, Miroslav," said Roy Carpenter in a strangled voice, "I don't know what you're talking about. It was those ecology nuts. Ask the police, they'll tell you."

Lukjovic's pale old eyes stared at the young sergeant. "No. Perhaps I tell you, Carpenter. I tell you how this happen. Natalia, she find out something maybe, like how you work in Bosnia helping drugs transit to West. Perhaps she learn this from people back home, in Pale, that something smell bad in International Police Force. That Canadian, this Carpenter smell bad." The old man nodded. "Yes, she find out something when she start make contact with people. She find out. So you kill her."

Carpenter felt his neck would snap from being forced backward by the strong man standing behind him. But with the knife blade firmly against his throat, the alternative was too horrible to contemplate. "It was those environmentalists, I tell you. She was being threatened by those wackos. I saw the notes."

"Yes, yes. You clever, Carpenter. This give you good

idea, yes? You security man. You RCMP. You know about these threats. So you make seal joke, yes? You make these threats from *wackos*"—he rolled this new word around in his mouth—"come true. And same for other man, fur seller, I think. You kill him to make police believe this also ecology killing."

"You've got this all wrong, Miroslav."

"You know," said Lukjovic, "at first I like you. When you start—helping me—when you start working as my boy in narcotics branch at RCMP, I think, here is boy I can trust. I trust him in Ottawa, and he work for me in Bosnia. Everything fine. You come to London. So I even think, this man, he can keep special eyes on my daughter. Keep her safe. What then, security man?"

Carpenter tried his last gambit. "Miroslav, it's true that she found out about me. But she had found out about *both* of us. She saw us together, you see, in Montreal. At one of your parties a couple of years ago. When I was working undercover for the narcotics branch, when you and I first became—associates. Then after my time in Bosnia—where I did good work for you, Miroslav, you know I did—I came to London. She recognized me. She asked how I knew you. Of course I told her she was mistaken, that I didn't know you at all."

Carpenter could scarcely get his words out. His voice was making curious gurgling noises, and his words were uttered in short, violent explosions, but he had no choice but to continue. "She was suspicious, I guess. Started following up. She must have heard something about the drug operation. I know she got in touch with people in Pale. She pieced together enough information to ruin me, to ruin *us*, Miroslav. She confronted me. She was upset, about us, about the operation. About what your involvement would do to her career. She threatened to turn me in, no matter the harm to herself or to you. You have to understand, Miroslav, you would have gone down with me. It would only have been a matter of time. I did you a favor, Miroslav. I did both of us a favor."

Miroslav Lukjovic leaned back on the hard wooden chair. "You did me favor, yes? Kill my daughter because she smarter than you. Why you not call me? Tell me what happens? I could talk to her, stop her do this thing. But no, you make so-called ecology killing. Kill my Natalia instead. And other man, too. Innocent fur man. You coward, Carpenter."

"Please, Miroslav. Please." He was choking. "I had no choice."

Lukjovic shrugged his shoulders. "As you say, no choice. But thank you for confession. I am sorry I have no seal club. Just regular knife. What to do." Lukjovic nodded slightly at his associate.

The man sliced through Carpenter's vocal cords.

Of course they were too late. So were the local patrol cars they had radioed to get to the scene immediately. Now yellow crime scene tape was strung across the entrances to the block of flats, and across Carpenter's door. The scene inside was ghoulish enough, but what Liz found the most jarring was that Sergeant Carpenter, sitting slumped in a chair with his throat slashed wide open, was proudly attired in his full dress uniform.

ELEVEN

Sergeant Gilles Ouellette was at Heathrow for the third time within the last two weeks and had long since lost the battle with chronic jet lag. Wilkins was not in much better shape, having slept at best two hours before waking to meet the 7:30 AM plane from Ottawa. Ouellette was sorely disappointed when Wilkins related the events of the previous night—events in which Ouellette would have loved to play a part but had missed entirely. At the time of the Carpenter murder and the late-night capture of Lukjovic, he had been cramped in economy class, watching some dumb romantic comedy and struggling with a faulty headset.

"Cheer up, mate," said Wilkins, as they waited at the baggage carousel. "If it hadn't been for the information you phoned in, we'd never have pieced things together."

Ouellette, slightly cheered by this, scanned the conveyor belt for signs of his luggage.

"We picked up Lukjovic and his henchman, some guy named Adam Mikievic, here at the airport," Wilkins continued. "Well, when I say 'we,' I mean that an army of cars descended on this place once we put out the word. Not to mention the roadblocks and the rest; it was one hell of an operation. Anyway, Lukjovic and Mikievic were trying to buy tickets to Belgrade. They're in custody now, although Lukjovic wasn't saying much when I left. He was pretending he didn't understand English, so we brought in an interpreter, but he is still keeping quiet. At least that was the case at about three o'clock this morning, when the boss sent me home for some sleep. He and your inspector were still trying to get something out of him."

"What about this—henchman—as you say?" asked Ouellette with one eye on the rapidly thinning crowd at the carousel.

"Hay and Forsyth seemed to think they could get him to talk, although they weren't convinced that he knew very much."

"They're lost, aren't they?" asked Ouellette a bit sadly.

"Hay and Forsyth?" asked Wilkins, surprised. "Why, no,

I don't think so. I mean, I know they act a bit funny around each other sometimes, but frankly, *I* think that's because—"

"Not Hay and Forsyth," sighed Ouellette. "My bags. They're lost. Come on, let's get to the missing baggage counter. I can do this in my sleep."

If Ouellette felt unsuitably dressed when he arrived at Scotland Yard in his travel clothes—jeans and a Labatt Blue sweatshirt—he was even more taken aback when he saw Hay and Forsyth. They were dressed up for a party, and it looked like it had been a particularly rough one. Hay was, or at least had been, in black tie. The bow tie and tuxedo jacket had long ago been discarded and tossed carelessly on a nearby chair. Hay had rolled the sleeves of his quality dress shirt up onto powerful forearms, and his collar was open. A night's growth of beard was hardly consistent with the formal attire. Seven or eight used styrofoam cups were stacked up next to him on the desk, a half-full one in his hand.

Ouellette's own boss looked even stranger for eight o'clock in the morning, if that were possible. She was wearing a rather crumpled black cocktail dress, which had probably looked quite nice twelve hours ago. Her RCMP jacket was slung about her shoulders, and much of her hair had escaped from the large gold clip clamped on her head. Her makeup was smudged, her eyes quite black. The high heels completed the picture. *Looks like she's been dragged in by Vice*, Ouellette thought to himself with a grin, but of course he said nothing.

"Good God," said Wilkins, "you never got home at all?"

"No," said Hay in a voice thick with exhaustion. "The thug started talking earlier this morning, and then we couldn't shut him up. We just finished a little while ago. We were waiting for you lads to get in so we could get out of here and get some sleep."

Forsyth turned her red-rimmed eyes to her young sergeant. "You've had an update, then?" she asked. Ouellette nodded. "You did great work. The implications of all this are staggering. We can expect a full-scale inquiry when we get home."

"I wouldn't be surprised if they put you in charge after all this," said Ouellette.

"Please, don't threaten me now," she said. "I'm not up to it." She was exhausted. "All I want is some sleep."

They arranged to meet back there later in the afternoon to swap notes and piece things together. Hay drove Liz to her hotel. Unusual for them, they rode in almost complete silence, too tired to smoke let alone converse. It was raining again, and Liz found the now-familiar slap of Hay's windshield wipers somehow comforting. They were both exultant about the night's work but too exhausted to enjoy it. Hay left her at the door with a quiet "Now get some sleep, Forsyth," and she wasn't inclined to argue. By the time she got inside her room—the empty little bottle of

Ballantine's still on the nightstand—she was incapable of coherent thought. She tossed the new dress and shoes into a corner and slept.

Shortly after five o'clock that afternoon, the four reconvened. Liz still felt a bit sleepy and dazed but was shocked awake by Wilkins, who said, "I'm afraid we've had some bad news. Paul Rochon called earlier to inform us that Mary Kellick was found dead in her apartment this morning. Suicide, it seems. Several bottles of some type of antidepressant next to her. It's being checked out, of course, but there doesn't seem to be much doubt. Rochon thought we ought to know."

Hay slumped back in his chair. "I guess we should have seen that coming."

Liz was stunned and felt an overwhelming sadness about the death of a woman she hardly knew. "We knew that she was fragile and very upset about the Guévin murder. Perhaps we could have done something . . ." But she knew there was nothing they could have done, and it wasn't their place to do so anyway. Surely someone at the High Commission could have helped this unhappy girl?

"I don't think there's anything anyone could have done, Forsyth," said Hay, reading her thoughts. "I expect this has been on the cards for some time."

They were silent for a while. Liz felt as though she was surrounded by death. Most of the lives lost had been innocent ones. Mary Kellick, she thought, had been something of a small, defenseless animal herself. Liz wondered suddenly if Sharon Carruthers might have had something to do with Kellick's suicide. She wouldn't have been at all surprised.

As for Natalie Guévin, Liz reflected, she had been a decent person who happened to learn too much. Liz couldn't bring herself to waste much pity on Carpenter; he had been a disgrace. But Lester Wilmot had only been a convenient target, an innocent in no way connected with other events. And Mrs. Wilmot was surely another victim, alone now in her tidy little home with the dried flower wreath on the front door.

"So what about Cox then?" asked Ouellette. "He had nothing to do with anything?"

Hay answered, toying with a recently drained cup. "He did send the threats to both Guévin and Wilmot, and to God knows how many others. He said as much, and we can have him for that. I'm also thinking seriously of charging him with wasting police time and perhaps impeding an investigation. He committed no murder, but he didn't go out of his way to defend himself. In fact, he deliberately strung us along, making us believe he had no alibi for the second killing. It was the publicity he wanted all along, you see. Anything to keep his name and Eco-Action in the papers." Hay shook his head in disgust.

"Remember how quickly the papers put the two crimes

together," Hay asked, "and made the so-called environmental connection? I'll bet you any money that was down to Cox. As I say, he committed no murder, but he was more than happy to come along for the ride."

Liz was still thinking about Mary Kellick. "I still wish it had been Sharon Carruthers," she muttered. "She deserves locking up. And it's hard to blame Wesley Carruthers for falling for Natalie when he had *that* to come home to every night."

The two younger men nodded vigorously in agreement. Hay reflected for a moment, then remarked, "I still find it deplorable that Carruthers was willing to collude in his wife's slander against Natalie Guévin. Remember, Natalie had already had to cope with that kind of character assassination from the weasel Jarvis when she was alive. The same thing happens to her after she's gone, with the tacit approval of her lover." He shook his head as if to clear his thoughts and continued, "But it was you, Forsyth, who made the Bosnia connection and got us on the right track."

Wilkins picked up the thread. "In the so-called Bosnia connection, then, Lahaie was the odd man out, right? He had nothing to do with any of it?"

Hay said, "That's right. He was a victim of rumor and suspicion fueled by previous problems in the Canadian military. That's all. His nose is clean. Again."

Liz smiled to herself. She always found Hay's reaction to whom he described as "the dashing colonel" somewhat amusing. She said, "What I want to know, Hay, is how you put two and two together so quickly last night—God, was it only last night?—and figured out that Carpenter might be in trouble."

Hay wandered over to the coffee pot and absently picked up another cup. He was trying to remember when he'd last had a meal. "Well, of course I wasn't sure. It was pretty sketchy at that point. But the possible connection between the drugs and Carpenter and Lukjovic was by then established by Sergeant Ouellette's good work in Ottawa. It struck me that perhaps Guévin had figured something out. And it was you, Forsyth, who saw Lukjovic at the reception, seemingly looking for someone. He had mentioned something about 'unfinished business,' remember?"

Liz nodded.

"And then he left," Hay continued. "None of us saw Carpenter last night, so I wondered if Lukjovic might not have been after him."

"And this drug operation, then," said Wilkins, "Carpenter and Lukjovic were working together?"

"Not exactly," said Liz. "It seems that Carpenter was working *for* Lukjovic. We finally started getting some information out of Lukjovic's goon, Mikievic, early this morning. He started spilling the beans when we told him his landed immigrant status in Canada could be revoked if he didn't talk."

"Could it?" asked Ouellette, interested.

"Damned if I know," replied Liz, "but it worked like a charm. Mikievic claims that, in fact, it was Lukjovic himself who slit Carpenter's throat, and that he knew nothing of their dealings until last night. I don't much believe him on either score. He's big, he's tough, and he's much more likely to be capable of subduing Carpenter than the old man would be.

"Anyway, his story goes something like this. I'm filling in a few blanks here, but I think it's pretty accurate. For most of his time in Canada, Lukjovic was an honest businessman with a highly successful string of dry-cleaning establishments. Things started to change, though, when the situation began heating up in his homeland. He started cultivating Carpenter when Carpenter was working undercover in the RCMP narcotics branch. I expect Lukjovic got to know him casually, then started inviting him to dinners, parties. You know the routine. Eventually he bought Carpenter off, and Carpenter started feeding him information from RCMP files.

"Lukjovic was already into the drug game by then, and Carpenter's information helped him stay out of trouble. When Carpenter was posted to the International Police Task Force in Bosnia, it was like manna from heaven for Lukjovic. He had a man, his own man, well placed on the ground to facilitate the illegal transfer of drugs out of Bosnia and into Canada. An ardent Serbian nationalist, Lukjovic could then recoup the profits and use them to help finance the regime back home."

"And Natalie Guévin figured this out by herself?" asked Ouellette. "She must have been quite an investigator in her own right."

"She was," acknowledged Hay, "but don't forget, she knew her father and his politics. This Adam Mikievic said that apparently Natalie had seen Carpenter in company with her father some time ago, and had recognized Carpenter when he arrived in London as the RCMP liaison. Something must have struck her as odd, and she started checking. Remember that Carruthers told us she had been making contact with people in Bosnia and was extremely preoccupied? And that she spent an afternoon with a cousin from Pale who was passing through London? It must have been about that time that things started falling into place for her."

Liz continued, "So whether she confronted Carpenter with facts or just suspicions we'll probably never know. It was enough to frighten him into killing her, anyway. And he, as one of the High Commission's key security personnel, would have known about the death threats she had received and about the anti-sealing campaign. He was also someone who could roam the High Commission and Residence premises at will, at any time, without alerting suspicion. As such, he would have had easy access to her appointment book and would have known that Dr. Cox was expected on Thursday afternoon.

"Carpenter staged what seemed to be a murder by an environmental madman. He was clever, I'll give him that. He must have brought the ax handle and knife to the office in his gym bag. He was something of an athlete after all and probably carried the bag around with him all the time. Knives and axes are not all that difficult to come by in London, as we know all too well. He would have lured her into the anteroom—the one with the white carpet, for effect—perhaps on the grounds that he wanted to talk to her about her father. He probably waited for her to enter, making sure at the same time that no one else wandered into the dining room, and knocked her unconscious from behind. Then he killed her, leaving poor Mary Kellick to find the body." Liz slumped backward, out of breath.

Hay added, "The knife is probably at the bottom of the Thames by now, along with a lot of other murder weapons. As for the second killing, that of Lester Wilmot, it was solely Carpenter covering his tracks. He may have panicked, or it might have been thought through in advance. In any event, he was keen to ensure the environmental link wasn't missed, to ensure the eco-warriors were in the frame. He couldn't have known that Cox was more than willing to do that for him."

He continued, "Remember that Mrs. Wilmot told us her husband had visited the High Commission to report the harassment he was facing from the eco-warrior types? For all we know, he may have spoken directly to Carpenter, which was all Carpenter needed to stage the second murder. It's quite easy, murder, once you know how. Or so I'm told," he added quickly when he saw Liz's quizzical glance.

Wilkins interjected, "And wasn't it Carpenter who identified the ax handle as the kind used to kill baby seals? He didn't want us to miss the connection."

"That's absolutely right," agreed Liz. "When Lukjovic came here to retrieve the body, he must have started putting two and two together himself. After all, he had more information than we did to start with. Carpenter was away for a couple of days, so Lukjovic, on the pretext of 'unfinished business,' waited for him to return. And murdered him in retribution for the killing of his daughter."

Wilkins whistled. "So that's it," he said. "Simple, isn't it?" He thought for a moment. "And Carpenter, of course, was in an ideal position to cover his tracks. He would just be part of the woodwork as far as the security personnel were concerned."

"And to think," added Ouellette, "that bastard was even taking notes for us during some of the interviews." He was appalled that someone who wore the same uniform as he did could commit such atrocities.

"Never, ever trust a Mountie," said Hay gravely.

Liz was about to react when she realized it was supposed to be a joke.

"And now, there's a great deal of paperwork to be done," said Hay and was greeted by a general groan from the others.

Wilkins opened his notebook, while Ouellette looked with dismay at a stack of forms in the middle of the table. DCI Hay watched Inspector Forsyth search for a pen in her purse.

"Liz," said Hay abruptly.

"Yes?" she asked, startled by the sound of her first name. He always called her Forsyth.

"I believe," he said, looking at her intently, "that you and I might, perhaps, have some unfinished business of our own."

She was locked in his intense gaze, slightly immobilized. "Perhaps—you might be right," she replied, her voice a bit unsteady.

"I believe we said the Bull's Head, didn't we?" he asked, rising but keeping his eyes fixed on hers.

"I believe we did," she agreed, allowing herself to be propelled toward the door without a backward glance.

Ouellette and Wilkins watched them leave the room. Wilkins turned to Ouellette, raising his eyebrows and shooting him a quizzical glance. Ouellette didn't know the answer to that particular question, although he had been wondering the same thing. He shook his head slightly and shrugged his shoulders. They started on their paperwork.

ACKNOWLEDGMENTS

A great many thanks are due to Ruth Linka and her professional and dedicated team at TouchWood Editions in Victoria for giving me the opportunity to publish my crime fiction story. I am especially grateful for the expertise, informed comment, and great support of my editor, Frances Thorsen.

For their generosity in sharing their expertise in their fields, I owe a great debt to RCMP Chief Superintendant Lynn Twardosky (ret'd) and coroner Barbara McLintock.

I am very grateful for the love and support of my brother, Clifford Wilkinson, and his family, and for the great encouragement and thoughtful suggestions of my dear friends Ian Hill, Alison Green, Ann Cronin-Cossette, Frank Haigh, and many others too numerous to mention here. You know who you are.

I owe more than I can possibly acknowledge to my sister-in-law, Chantal Ouellette, who was there at the inception of the story, who continues to encourage and assist me in my writing, and whose generosity with the red wine resulted in an outline for the second book.

Finally, I would like to thank Margaret Bechard and Nicola Furlong for lighting a fire under me and making me believe that this could happen.

Before taking to crime writing, JANET BRONS worked as a foreign affairs consultant following a seventeen-year career in the Canadian foreign service, with postings in Kuala Lumpur, Warsaw, and Moscow. She has also been a researcher in the Alberta Legislature and at the House of Commons. Janet holds a master of arts in political science and international relations.